HARD BOILED

Books by Kathryn Elizabeth Jones

HARD BOILED

A Susan Cramer Mystery

Book 3

KATHRYN ELIZABETH JONES

Idea Creations Press
www.ideacreationspress.com

 Idea Creations Press
www.ideacreationspress.com

Library of Congress Control Number: 2016947334

ISBN-13: 9780996665780
ISBN-10: 0996665781

Printed in the U.S.A.

Acknowledgments

A huge thank you to my beta readers: Bethany Wursten, Tricia Leslie and Ali Gordon and to my cheerleader and *write* hand man, Douglas Jones.

A hard-boiled cozy mystery usually means an R-rated cozy, but not in *this* case. As each of my mysteries reflect some sort of 'egg' theme, such was also the case with Hard Boiled. Rather than hard-boiled material, (you will find all of my material G or PG rated) expect a bit of sleuthing regarding family and the hard heads they typically wear.

Kathryn

Prologue

So, you're married?" The words from her mother whirled themselves into Susan's ear almost strangling her. Someone—*something* had leaked the news. No mention had been made in the paper. No call had been made by her. And now...

"Well, yes, I'm married. He's a good man..."

"That cop."

"His name is Henry."

Susan could hear talking in the distance.

"We need to see you. Something has happened to your...Bob."

Henry was leaning over her and kissing her neck. The attention was soothing; it almost made her forget that her mother was talking about Bob. Something had happened to him?

"So, how many hours will it take you to get here?"

"Hours? We decided to get a hotel nearby before returning home. We're only a few minutes from you." The kissing continued. She was melting.

"You're staying at a hotel? Why didn't you ask to stay here? Anyway, what's that noise?" her mother finally asked.

She might have asked the same thing of her mother. She was not alone—either.

"Nothing, Mother. Bob?"

"Oh yes. He...he. I can't even say it."

A pause, far longer than Susan would have wished to make it, pushed itself between the lines. What would her mother say now? That her ex had somehow found someone else to marry? That he was ill, in the hospital? Susan was not prepared for what came next, but how could anyone be prepared to hear such disturbing news?

"What is it, Mom? What's happened?"

She could hear talking again in the distance and then silence.

"Bob, your...Bob has killed himself," her mother said.

***

"When did you get the couch cleaned?" Susan asked. It looked suddenly whiter than she remembered it, though the fabric seemed to be the same. Henry sat next to her on the stark white sofa and tried to look interested. Perhaps he was interested, his eyes opening wide, looking around the room of relatives.

Her older sister, Kate, wore sparkling red shoes to complement her tight jeans and red top, and mother's new husband, William, sat nearby, brushing at some imagined hair on his almost bald head. His hair might have once been black or brown...and he didn't resemble in the slightest her father, he was definitely a different man, in every way, shape and form.

"Just last week, though I had to clean it again when..." Her words stopped like they'd hit against a wall. Everyone was silent. "He died...there." She pointed her thin and wrinkled finger.

"Here? Where I'm sitting?" Susan stood and looked down at the couch. Henry followed suit. They must have looked like a couple of stooges. Her mother, Hope, whose own hair was now a woven gray on muted red, smiled over at her husband. "You're right. Susan, sit. It's okay, the spill has been cleaned up."

So that's what blood was. A spill.

Susan's heart pounded. How had her ex-husband died? Even now, she was sitting on the spot where he'd been stabbed or shot. Blood was hard to get out of upholstery no matter the elegance of the material. She could hardly stand it. In that brief second, she was glad no one could see into her mind. They would think her shallow at best. Shouldn't she be sad that her ex-husband had a... passed? But crazy enough she did feel something. No matter *how* Bob had died it was as if her own blood ran chill.

"When?" she asked. "When did Bob die?"

Her mother paled. She wiped a thin hand across her hair, almost matching the movement her new husband had offered moments previous. How long had the two been married? Long enough, it seemed.

"A week and a half ago we tried to reach you, but you were still on that cruise and going through some wrapping up, I guess. The funeral was last week."

Susan remembered the last few days before leaving the *Aloha* and finally returning home. Henry had turned off her cell phone; *a real honeymoon was in order*, he'd said. And though Susan had seen the calls she hadn't listened to the voice messages or made any attempts to return them. Not even after returning home. She would have never known what had happened to Bob if her mother hadn't continued to hound her.

"We were all in the back room, all except Bob. 'Television was in order' he'd said and we'd all left him—alone—and spoke with each other in another room where we wouldn't disturb him. We weren't gone but half an hour when we heard a sound from down the hall.

"Your...Bob was so depressed. He kept talking about how much he missed you and that when you returned home he was going to make it work. And then, that funny call came, telling us that you'd just gotten married. We thought Bob could handle it.

"And that night, he said, 'Let me watch a show, I need to be alone.' And that was it. Next we knew William was coming into the room...and..."

Susan sat. Finally.

Henry reached for her hand.

"That's where we found him. He had been complaining for hours about his sick stomach, throwing up. We thought he had a terrible flu. He said he was tired and had a headache. We even wondered if he'd gotten himself drunk. He'd been talking as if he was. He was on the couch and the mixture in his cup was all over everything."

"The mixture?" Henry asked, for Susan was silent. Her throat had closed off.

"The police are calling it poisoning," Kate offered, her long nails hovering over her jeans. "He'd evidently mixed Gatorade with antifreeze and..."

"Seriously?" Susan was in shock.

"Dead...serious," William said, catching himself. "Sorry," he added lamely, brushing his head of baldness.

Hope lifted a piece of paper from the end table. The note was in a sheet protector. "This is for you," she said, peering into Susan's eyes. "He left it for everyone, perhaps, but mostly for you. We wouldn't have been able to get this at all if police hadn't already discounted suicide as the cause of death." She revealed a piece of paper, folded over—once.

Dear family,
You will Think me weak but I don't care. life is meaningless. I Haven't anyone to love, not really. I sit for days on end hoping she'll Come back to me, but she won't. I know That now. I hope she is Happy. I hope I will be—where I'm going.
Please Understand. I love my family. Even Though you are really not my family anymore. Thank you for taking me In, but I have to leave you now.
bob

The note was handwritten in Bob's scrambled scrawl; capitals where lower case letters should have been and vise versa. She couldn't stand it.

"This is—it?"

Her mother reached for her hand. Susan pulled it back. "Bob wouldn't do this, any of this!" A tear formed now, in her left eye and she was surprised. "Bob might have been depressed, but he would NEVER kill himself. NEVER!"

Henry jumped at her side but he was as silent as death.

"It says here..."

"I know what is says, Mother. What did Bob know about poisoning, huh? And like he said, he'd been waiting for me, wait-ing" the words choked in her throat, "Why would he suddenly give up...NOW?"

"Because, daughter, you were married."

She stood, yanking Henry's arm from around her shoulder though she hadn't noticed it there until now. "He DIDN'T kill himself and I'll prove it."

"PROVE IT?" Now Kate was in an uproar. "HOW for heaven's sake."

"I don't know HOW, but I'll do it, like before." She shouldn't have said the words, but there, they were out. Henry sat on the couch solemnly as she raved, her sister's face burned a red hot fire engine color matching her shirt. Her mother?

12

She was standing there her face like a hot iron skillet. "You don't know anything—Susan. You haven't been here. You don't know anything about what's been going on—"

"So then, tell me, TELL ME, Mother. I'm waiting."

"Bob wasn't the same after you left. I was worried about him. You should have been worried about him."

Susan rolled her eyes. "He's a grown man, Mother. Why should I be worried?"

Tears glistened in Hope's eyes. "Because..."

"Well?"

"I'm just too fired up right now. Maybe later." A tear rolled down her mother's cheek as she turned from her and retreated into the kitchen.

Susan gaped at her. She stood in the same position for at least two minutes before she sat down again. No matter. She was going to solve this murder, no matter what.

Time

Susan was visibly shaking. She had no idea what had gotten into her. Sure, she'd cared about Bob in a sort of off-hand, *now we're divorced* kind of way. But cry? And rant and rave over his death not being suicide? She had no proof that he hadn't killed himself. No proof at all. So why the hysterics?

Henry was sitting by her at the foot of their bed. They'd had their honeymoon and everything had been beautiful. And now...this?

"Look. Let the police handle the situation."

"But the note..." The words trailed off from there and all Susan could do was blubber. "I—have to find the murderer."

"Why? How do you know he didn't commit suicide?"

"Because I know him, that's why." She pounded the bed with her left fist. The comforter, a black ensemble, still reeked of new fibers. "I mean, I used to know..."

"That's right. You used to know him. People can change, Susan."

"I know," she sniveled, "but he *blamed* me."

"Blamed you?"

"Yes. He wrote that note and blamed me for his death. How can I live with myself knowing I... killed him?"

"So that's it. But you didn't kill him, Susan. He killed himself. He was lonely, that's all."

"And so he killed himself? Not Bob."

"Okay, maybe you're right." He took her hand. She let him. "But Susan, honey, you don't need to go in search of the killer. My desk job..."

"Yes, that's right! You'll have an in, like always! You can talk to me about the case, fill me in on things. I don't even have to go inside the police station!"

"Really, Susan. I'm done with sleuthing. Besides, it wouldn't be honest. I need to stick with my job and leave it at that."

"But you know you'll be bored." She smiled over at him. He didn't smile back.

"Bored or not, this is our new life and you have the *Hotel Camaro* to worry about. And your friend, what's her name?"

"Jane."

"And those kids."

"Oscar and Brianne. I almost forgot."

"Of course you did, honey. Let me get you some lunch and we'll go about getting things prepared for tomorrow. We have a bit of a drive."

***

"I can hardly believe it! You're finally here!" Jane held Susan in the tightest grip she could manage without cutting off Susan's air supply. "And how is marriage?"

Susan couldn't help smiling. "He's a good man," she said. "Romantic, a bit stubborn and full of reasons why I should be here."

"And why shouldn't you be?" Jane Dove brushed her short brown hair from her full face.

"Something terrible has happened. Bob has been murdered."

"What?" Jane's face paled.

"Murdered. Poisoned."

"When?"

"While Henry and I were on our honeymoon."

She covered her mouth. "Wow. He's really...you know...gone?"

"Yes."

"I can't believe it. He was always calling over here and asking for you, but I never thought...Well, I don't believe it. Did he leave a note?"

"Yes."

"Suicide." Jane's eyes looked away.

"Bob wouldn't commit suicide."

Jane walked to the front desk, the same desk she'd sat behind just two months ago; same desk, but it was much more organized than when she had left it. And there was a young girl sitting behind it. *Brianne!*

The girl's light brown hair looked like it had been recently brushed. It glittered and static ends flew in various directions around her head. They embraced. "I thought you'd never come back," she said, jumping from the chair and taking her hand. "I'm 10 now."

"Her birthday was last week," Jane said. "I couldn't get her to wait even though she knew you'd be returning from your honeymoon."

"I bet you kissed," Brianne offered.

"Y-yes," Susan coughed. "And you? How have you been?"

"Oscar is stupid, but other than that, good."

Susan reflected on Brianne's 13-year-old brother and wondered how he was really doing, but figured the interrogation could wait until she was alone with him. "And your mother?"

"Dead."

"She passed just a few weeks ago."

"Jane!"

"Sorry I didn't tell you, but you were all geared up for the wedding festivities. I wanted you to have a good time without worries. I have been given temporary custody. No family members.

Suddenly, a *clunk* was heard from behind the front desk. A head bobbed.

"Oscar!"

"What?"

"Come here, let me see you!"

The boy stood. "Sorry," he said. "I hate stuff like this."

"Stuff like what?" Susan couldn't believe he'd been hiding behind the desk the entire time. She couldn't believe no one had said anything.

"I have used a couple of rooms here for the kids to sleep in," Jane said slowly as if waiting for the boy to speak.

"I should have waited for you for my birthday," said Brianne, taking Susan's hand suddenly, but she was beaming over at Jane.

The sound of afternoon traffic filtered through Susan's ears. Everything appeared the same as before except that two people had died and life had gone on here without her. Oscar didn't move and so Susan watched him from a short distance as he picked at his clothes, paying particular attention to something he must have dropped on the floor.

***

The briskness of fall was just opening when Susan felt like her bearings were returning to normal—whatever normal was. Henry had returned to work, her mother to worry and her sister, to all of those fancy things Susan had never been able to consciously consider. The case on her ex-husband was closed. There was no doubt that he'd taken his own life and she'd been told multiple times to move forward with her life as she'd done for months now, without him.

Henry was supportive, but something didn't feel right to Susan and it bothered her that the air smelled of death and her skin prickled at every sound that came from her mother's new husband. There was something about his manner, no, his eyes; dark, like the unending reaches of a cave. And when he looked at her, it was never at her, almost as if he'd built some sort of wall that she couldn't penetrate.

And now?

Now he was standing before her like some bald god. "So, say it," he said.

"Say what?"

"That you hate me. That I'll never be a father to you."

She peered up at him from the couch and watched his hands as they felt their way into the pockets of his trousers. The slacks were slick and perfect and expensive.

"I don't hate you, I..."

"Of course you do, Susan. And it's okay. We've just met and I probably will never hold a candle to your father."

Her father? Funny and perhaps not so funny, the thought of him taking the place of her father had never occurred to her. Her father was dead and he'd been gone long enough for her to move on. He wasn't a bit like him anyway...

"I don't hate you," she repeated. "It's just that..."

Her mother re-entered the living room with a tray of cookies. Susan had decided on a chair this time. She was alone without Henry and thoughts of sitting where Bob had previously died sent shivers up her spine.

"So, tell us about your wedding," Hope asked.

Susan reached for a cookie. "What do you want to know?" she asked.

"All of it."

"We were married in Kaanapali Beach in Maui."

"I bet that was beautiful," said her mother. "Wish I could have been there. What did you wear?" She took a bite of cookie and patted her lips with a napkin. William smiled eagerly at her, his dark eyes blinking.

"Just something I already owned."

"You can't mean you didn't buy a gown?" said her mother.

"No, I didn't buy a gown."

Her mother shifted uneasily in her chair. She was wearing a perfectly fitted pantsuit, just as if she'd just stepped forth from the 70s. Her hair, a gray-red now, yet held a certain elegant style as it swept forth from her face. "So, this Henry, is he the same cop who helped you out when you went to jail?" she asked.

"The same." She took a bite, trying not to choke. Why *had* she come?

"And he's the one who helped you find the murderer on that cruise ship."

"Of course."

"And now you want to find the murderer of your husband, even though he wasn't murdered."

"My ex-husband." Susan inhaled deeply. "Really, mother. Bob was murdered. He would never take his life."

"Well, for months he sat around here and whined at me. I tried to get him help but he kept saying, 'She'll come back to me, she'll come back.' That last day, the day we gave him some privacy so that he could think about killing himself, all I could think about was what you'd done."

"What *I'd* done?" Susan gasped.

William cleared his throat. "This isn't helping," he said.

Hope took a sip of punch. "Why couldn't you have been more like your sister," she said, setting the glass down and blinking over at her.

"So that's it." Susan stood, leaving her own cookie and drink on the end table. "I'm going. Now." Feelings were bubbling inside her faster than shaken soda. Why had she come? Well, to learn more about Bob, that's why. Her mother would never change and the man she'd married was practically her un-identical twin. Kate wasn't home now, but Susan felt as if her spirit still lingered, still smiled at her from the corner chair as she turned to leave them. She could almost feel her eyes on her.

"When did Kate leave for home?" she asked lamely, facing her mother who was still sitting.

"Just the other day. She was supposed to call you."

"Well, she didn't."

Her mother shrugged. "Maybe if you had a better relationship."

Tears stung at Susan's eyes. She'd made a mistake in coming here. Why hadn't she decided on Skype or text? That would have been much easier. Still, it was important that she visit her mother, not just to get the information she needed to find her ex-husband's killer, but to get a sense of how involved they'd really been in his life. And how could she do that electronically? Sure, her ex meant little to her, but judging from the long drive she'd just taken, perhaps he'd meant more to her than she'd thought.

* * *

October came and went like a breeze and before she knew it, Susan was wrapped into all the motherliness taking care of Brianne and Oscar could bring. The death of her ex-husband had put everything behind schedule including the paperwork for the adoptions. Well, except for the fact that it would be months yet before everything was finalized anyway.

The *Hotel Camaro* had been whipped into shape while she was gone, the children even happier than when she'd left them, and their growth in just two months far surpassing even her greatest dreams. It was simply amazing.

"It's like this," Jane said, "the children here need a place to crash, yes, but they need some stability, too. And love."

Susan agreed. Near one hundred and fifty children at various times of the day were making their way here and she wasn't sure how many more they'd be able to house—even on a temporary basis.

"I know we're only an emergency shelter situation and most of these kids will come and go like summer meets fall, but what happens when they return to the streets, to their abusive homes?"

"They know they can come back," Susan offered. "We'll just make sure they feel like we're here for them."

"And how may that be?" Jane asked, running her fingers through her short hair. "I mean, these kids—just yesterday I had to pull a fast one. Seems some of them think that drugs are okay in the rooms."

"Drugs?"

"Really, Susan. I'm dealing with all sorts of stuff here. That girl I hired, she's about as helpful as a one-armed orangutan."

"So, where is she?"

"Fired her just before your return. I'm sorry, I had to. She thought she knew everything, but would do nothing to help me. It was all talk and no action I'm afraid."

"I'm sorry."

"As well, you should be. If it wasn't for Brianne and Oscar helping out I would have been in the nut house by now."

"And the cook?"

Susan had hired a cook before leaving on her cruise and she'd hired a groundskeeper. These were hopefully still in place.

"Yes, we still have Ms. Pratt and Mr. Gobel, though I'm wondering if Mr. Gobel is doing anything but smelling the roses. Did you see the state of the lawn?"

"I hadn't noticed," Susan said honestly. "And anyway, isn't it better that we focus more on the children coming in?"

Jane breathed heavily. "Just since you've been gone our backers and many of our charitable donations have thinned. Seems like everyone is tight fisted these days, even for children."

Susan recalled the many corporations, grants and other individual contributors who had been put in place before she'd attempted to leave the *Hotel Camaro* for her well-needed vacation. Where were they now?

Jane paled. "I didn't want to bother you with any of this while you were gone," she said, reaching across the table and taking Susan's hand, "but you've got to know, some changes are going to need to happen—quick—or you're going to lose this place."

Susan wondered why Jane hadn't said anything right after her return from her honeymoon, but reconsidered the thought. Jane didn't do anything by standard and if the truth be known Jane was probably waiting for just the right moment to break the news. Coming home and finding an ex-husband dead was probably bad enough news until she'd finally begun to settle in.

Secrets

"I'm so sorry, honey."

Henry was reaching for her and she could hardly stand the thought of telling him she was a failure. How could she have left Jane for two months to fight the battle alone? How could she have thought that she could handle the place without her? But she had handled it, for the most part, the building was still standing and more and more children were finding shelter there. So why did she feel so crummy?

"You'll get things worked out. Just give yourself some time."

But she didn't have time, at least not much. After spilling her guts about the leaky roof and the clogged plumbing, Jane had ventured into the subject of Oscar's new habits. Evidently, he'd been hanging out with some gang.

"Maybe it's time to close up shop," she said.

"What? And let your dream go? What about your lemon, raspberry and cinnamon pastries?"

Susan laughed. They'd been the first things she'd thought about after taking on the *Hotel Camaro* as the place where all children would be cared for and sheltered. But maybe that was it. "What do you think about the name?" she asked.

Sitting down at the kitchen table he plunked the round pizza pan in front of her. It was eight o'clock and she'd finally managed to get herself home, promising Jane that she would look for new help the following day and get on the plumbing and roof problems—something that would need to be fixed—yesterday.

"I have wondered about that," Henry said, sitting down and pouring them both some drinks. "Why would you want such a great place with a loser name like *Hotel Camaro* attached to it?"

Her heart skipped a beat but she said nothing.

"Really, Susan, that old place used to house drug addicts, prostitutes and thieves, perhaps it's time for a new name."

Sort of like *Gypsies, Tramps and Thieves*, Susan thought briefly and then she remembered the drug incident that Jane had told her about and nodded her head. "You're right, it's time for a new name, a new beginning. And I think I know just the one."

***

Honesty House. It was a good, clean name, one that would speak volumes to those who passed by the building and those who entered its doors. She liked it and so did Henry. Even Jane smiled when she heard the news and grinned even wider when Susan told her she'd schedule some interviews after the plumber finished.

But things, shall we say, have a strange way of turning out, even with the most detailed of plans. It started just after the plumber had left and she'd dialed the roofer who said he'd come over on Tuesday to bid for the project. Susan looked up front the front desk of the newly labeled *Honesty House* to see her sister, Kate, standing before her.

She was wearing black.

"I need to speak to you," Kate said as Susan gaped at her. Her sister looked a disheveled mess; her hair brushed but not styled. Susan could hardly take it in. It looked as if her sister had thrown on the first thing she'd come to in her closet and had run out the door. But she'd had to take a plane, too. And where were her bags?

"What's wrong? Is it mother?"

"One could only hope." Kate took a deep breath and continued. "I just can't do it, Susan. I can't. I can't work. I can't sleep. I can't..."

Susan left the counter and walked around to face her sister. With her arms wrapped around her sister's small form the girl began to weep. "I can't live with myself," she sobbed.

Kate trembled in her arms. Her sister had actually left her corporate life and had come to see her—her. It was beyond belief. And yet, her sister wouldn't have come, especially to her, if something heavy hadn't been weighing on her mind. But what?

"You will hate me," she sniffed, "just hate me, but I can't do this."

"Do what?" Her sister, still in her arms, sniffed once more then pulled herself away. She wasn't wearing any make-up either; a sorry sight for someone so far bent on making herself perfect. But she wasn't perfect now.

"Your husband...I mean your...Bob. He was murdered."

***

Henry paced the floor. "You mean to tell me that you know who murdered Bob?"

Kate trembled. "I think so," she said.

Henry reached for Susan's hand and together they sat across from the sister who had rarely been a sister to Susan. But now, like the time she'd bailed Susan out of jail, she was here, just when things couldn't get any worse.

"Bob was driving his roommates crazy. They had kicked him out months before, telling him he was 'a slob' and other things I'd rather not mention. When he came over to beg to live with Mom..." Kate said the word 'Mom' as if it was a real struggle, "...she caved. I couldn't believe it. After about an hour of talking to her it was if she was taking in her own boy instead of her son-in-law. I couldn't believe it."

"I can." Susan reflected over the many times she might have kicked her ex-husband out but didn't, she thought about all of the ways he'd continued to weasel his way into her life even after she'd left him; those whom he'd made friends with to watch her and so on. Bob could find himself in any situation he really wanted access to. "Look, Bob was a master at getting what he wanted and maybe he was finally beaten when he couldn't get me."

"Maybe. But Susan..." She placed her red finger nails, the only red on her person that Susan could see, on the table in front of her. With an occasional click of nails on wood, she told her and Henry the story:

"Just a few days after you... Bob came to live with Mom, she started acting sort of strange. It was just over the phone, I had loads of paperwork to do and couldn't be taken away from it—but one night near 2 a.m. she called me at my place. I remember looking at the clock and thinking, 'Mom must be hurt or something to call me so late,' but when I picked up the phone she didn't say anything. I kept asking her why she'd called and what she wanted but I heard nothing on the other end and so I finally hung up and called her back, but she didn't answer. The next morning, I called her again. She answered but denied that she'd attempted to call me early that morning."

Kate took a deep breath and continued: "She did tell me, however, that she'd met a nice man by the name of William that had finally begun to fill her heart with joy. I think she said, 'he is the joy of my life,' or something sentimental like that. Anyway, she spoke in glowing terms about her new man and I wondered then, just as I do now, if he was the one to call me that morning."

"Why would he do that?" Henry asked.

"When I finally visited a few days before Bob was murdered, he looked at me real funny and stared at me from across the dinner table."

"Well, you are beautiful," Susan said.

Kate didn't even blush. "Well, I know, but I don't think that was it. It was almost as if he wanted something from me—besides the obvious, if you know what I mean."

Susan blinked. Henry leaned in. "So, what you're saying is that the man makes you feel uncomfortable."

"Well, yes, but if it hadn't been for the episode that occurred just a day before Bob's passing, I might not have given the call or the stares a second thought."

Susan's heart stopped.

"Mom told me it didn't mean anything, William was just getting to know the place, checking out the cupboards, seeing what she had in the fridge, you know, snooping, but it still gives me the creeps whenever I think about it."

"What?" Susan asked.

"He was in the garage looking over a gallon of antifreeze."

"Maybe he needed it, for the car," Susan suggested, hoping against all hope that her sister was wrong.

"That's what I thought, too, but he only looked at it briefly, then sat it back down on the shelf and returned to the house. A few days later when it was discovered that anti-freeze and Gatorade had killed Bob I just got sick about it. I went to William privately and told him what I'd seen. He laughed at me, said I had an active imagination and that Bob could have retrieved the coolant as easily as he could have. Besides, what motive would he have of killing him?"

"He said that?" Henry asked.

"Yes, he looked right at me and said he had no motive for killing him other than he was a terrible house guest."

"So, you think William killed him?"

Kate wiped at her eyes. "Why not? He practically admitted it."

"Did you tell the police?" Susan asked.

"Of course not. I couldn't I..."

"What?" Henry prodded.

"I just couldn't. Let's just leave it at that," Kate said.

***

With Kate asleep in the guest room, she and Henry had time to talk. It was strange, really, her sister flying to her place to tell her something she might have shared over the telephone. Stranger still, that she'd come all this way without a suitcase; without even a change of clothing.

"I'm worried," Susan said, taking another sip of cocoa. "I mean, it isn't like Kate to get so riled up about anything. I know she came to the jail, but even then, she was firm and to the point, something her job as director of human resources has taught her."

"You're still hung up on that one?" Henry asked, stirring his own cocoa with a spoon.

"What one?"

"You know, my sister is the rich one, I am the poor one."

"Is it that obvious? Sorry. She just gets to me, you know. Until today, it's been all about her, all about her money, all about her job, all about her looks. She's perfect, you know."

"Was..." her husband offered, taking a sip. "I think it's interesting that she believes Bob has been murdered. And what if she isn't telling the truth? What reason would she have for lying?"

"She wouldn't as far as I'm concerned. The man had no money, nothing of worth to speak of that Kate would want. The only reason she'd come this far to tell me anything is because she felt she had to."

"So, what if William killed Bob?"

"Then we have a murder to solve."

"I'll go through some files tomorrow. See if I can find anything on him. In the meantime, once you're through at the *Hotel*...I mean

Honesty House tomorrow, we'll need to be making a trip over to your Mother's."

"What about Kate?"

"I think it's best she stays here."

***

"I'm going with you," she said. "I have to confront William."

"No, you're not. You're going to stay here where it's safe."

The woman paled. "You don't think..."

"I don't think anything," Susan lied. "I just want you to be safe." She looked into her sister's eyes. It was near 10 a.m., Susan should have been at work practically two hours ago, but her sister was still crying, still venting, still demanding that she come along.

"After work I'll be heading over, you can come with me to work if you'd like and I'll drop you off back here on my way out."

Kate rolled her eyes, the first sign since she'd arrived that she was still thinking logically. "Remember that time Mom talked to you about that hard-boiled egg?" she asked.

"What?"

"You remember. Mom placed an egg in your hand. You asked, 'Is it hard-boiled?'"

"And she said it wasn't," Susan finished. "She said my marriage was hard boiled and that she wished I'd chosen scrambled or over easy."

"So that you could make your marriage into whatever you wished." Kate smiled, the first smile Susan had seen since coming to tell her that her ex had been murdered.

"Why are you telling me this now?" she asked. Her mother had always been a little strange, a little eccentric, a little too high and mighty and her sister, she never really cared two bits about her unless things got way out of hand—like now.

"I just think it's interesting," Kate said, slipping on a blouse and jeans that Susan had lent her. They were both a little large, but her sister didn't seem to care. "Your marriage with Bob is over, but you have a new one starting, one that you can make into anything you want."

"What's that's supposed to mean?" she asked.

"Just what I said." She zipped the jeans. "Have a belt?" she asked.

Susan found the belt hanging in the closet; she hadn't worn it in ages. Kate slipped it through the belt loops and buckled it at a notch she'd never personally used. Her sister looked up. "Well?" she asked.

"You look fine," she said, but in fact her sister looked terrific, would forever look terrific even if she had to wear a paper bag.

They reached *Honesty House* some twenty minutes later. The drive was just long enough to hear that her sister still held the job at Jenkins Fidelity, that she wasn't seeing anyone and that all of her thoughts of late (especially since she'd returned after the funeral) were of her. Would Henry be the right one? Would they be able to make their marriage work? And most of all, would they be able to discover the murderer of her ex?

Susan could feel a headache coming on but tried to shrug it off. If Kate knew how she really felt about her visit and revelation of her ex-husband, she might just hop on board the plane and fly home.

She dared not say it; it was terrible just to think of it. But Susan was scared. Not only for herself, but for her husband, for Kate and for her mother. William; had he really poisoned her ex-husband and if so, why? Could Bob have really been such a burden? Could William have felt pressured somehow, because another man, an ex-in-law, was living in his house?

At the door, Susan turned. "I want you to be nice to Jane," she said. "This girl has been through a lot since my cruise and I'm just beginning to bandage everything together. Got it?" Her words were firm, Susan knew it, but she also knew her sister. At the first opportune moment, she would hover over Jane and ask her all sorts of things, things probably better left unsaid.

"You must think me some monster," said her sister. "Really, Susan, I do work in human resources."

She had to bring that up.

Susan opened the door and the two of them filtered inside. Jane was at the desk, Brianne standing by her side holding a notebook. She smiled when she saw her. "Hey, Susan!" Dropping the notebook to the wood floor she raced to her. Susan was pleased, the hesitancy she'd felt earlier seemed to be gone. But where was Oscar?

"Jane said I could wait for you, but I've been waiting a really, really long time. Who's this?" The girl's eyes blinked up at her sister.

"This is Kate, my sister. She lives in Virginia."

"Wow," Brianne gasped.

"Hi," Kate said. She tousled the girl's hair.

Brianne frowned. "I just brushed it," she said.

"Sorry," Kate offered.

"That's okay. I've got a brush upstairs." She smiled up at Kate. "You're pretty," she said.

"Thank you. So are you."

"Really? I mean, Oscar doesn't think so, but he's only my brother."

Jane reached her hand out. "Glad to meet you," she said. "You hold a striking resemblance to your sister."

Susan felt the blood rising to her cheeks.

"Well, sister, what do you think?" Kate practically glowed, as if she'd always known this hidden truth. But the thought felt funny and a little uncomfortable to Susan. She was attractive in a dull sort of way—everyone on the planet knew she would never be able to outshine her sister. Jane was just being kind.

"I'm glad I finally get to meet you," Kate offered, shaking the woman's hand. "I've heard enough glowing terms about you to keep you in the black for life."

"Is that so?" Jane turned to Susan.

"Well, yes," Susan lied; actually, she had never spoken about Jane other than to tell her sister that she was the assistant.

Jane turned to Brianne. "Go get your brother," she said, waving her finger in the direction of the front door. "Tell him Susan is here."

"Do I have to?" the girl wheezed.

"Yes, you have to. Now, pronto."

Brianne stamped her foot and headed for the front door. "But I'll miss everything," she wailed. "Tell me what I miss when I get back," she added, before pushing open the door.

Once gone, Jane frowned. "Two girls are here waiting for their interviews."

Susan had forgotten. "I'm sorry," she said. "With my sister coming I..."

"Don't worry another second." Jane seemed suddenly okay about her forgetfulness, but Susan knew she'd have to do better. She was home after all, and sister or no sister, she'd have to step it up if she expected Jane to stick-it-out.

***

"What?" Henry was frantic.

"I told you. Kate demands to come."

"Why?"

"She thinks she can help."

"But that's crazy. Really, Susan. Your mother can't know that she is here."

"Why not?"

"Yes, why not?" Kate was suddenly poking her head around the bedroom doorway. She'd been in the bathroom only seconds before, a perfect opportunity, Susan thought, to tell her husband the new plan.

"I'm a big girl and can handle this," she said. "I can handle Mother."

Henry was furious. "I thought we'd talked about this," he said, his eyes glaring into those of his sister-in-law. I thought..."

"Well, you thought wrong, brother. The last thing I want to do while I'm here is to pretend that I'm not here. Mother doesn't need to know why I've come; I can just say that I decided to make a surprise visit to you—which is true, that I missed seeing you, which is also true and that I've come to...to... Well, I haven't figured that part out yet."

"Maybe missing me will be enough," Susan said.

"But we've just returned from our honeymoon," Henry offered, blushing the same color as his hair. "That's got to feel strange to Mother."

"I'll just say that I have some work here and I thought that I might spend some time with my sister while here."

"Not good enough," said Henry, pacing now. "What about a boyfriend?"

"Now that would be interesting." Kate smiled and placed her red nails against her matching lips. It was then Susan noticed the outfit change. Evidently, her sister had found some time while at *Honesty House* to escape for a little shopping. "I like it. I was with Mom and William a few days before the funeral and a couple of three days following it. I never spoke about seeing anyone but I wasn't with them 24/7."

"Come up with a name and a bit of facts about him that you'll remember. If she asks, you'll be prepared to say something."

***

William was more than a little annoyed. "If you'd prepared us for your visit, your mother could have been here. She's left for the day. Won't be back until tomorrow."

Susan was stunned. Her mother never went anywhere and especially not alone. "Where did she go?"

The man known as William brushed a hand over his bald head. "It's a secret," he said.

"A what?" Susan's heart pounded like a hundred horses.

"A secret." They were all still standing at the front door. William hadn't even offered to let them in. The daylight was narrowing and Susan's arms were cold.

"Look, I've got things to do. If you'll excuse me." Susan blinked as the door shut.

"Unbelievable," Kate said.

Susan was stunned, Henry silent. As they gaped at the door with the golden knocker, Henry knocked. In moments, they were all staring into the face of William. "And?" he asked.

"And we want to come in for a few moments. If that's alright with you."

"Like I said..." For a minute the man just stood there, staring at them all, his mouth pinched like a drying grape. And then he smiled. "Kate, so what brings you back here? Wasn't the funeral enough?"

The words were cold, shallow and a bit unbelievable to Susan. Who was this man anyway and where was his charm now, now that the woman in his life wasn't near him?

"I came back to visit my sister," was the reply.

"Not unannounced, I hope."

Kate didn't even flinch. "I've met someone," she said.

The man's mouth curled into a smile, but his eyes were still cold. "Figures. And you, Susan, shouldn't you be enjoying your new life with your new husband?"

Henry blinked. "When will Hope be returning?" he asked.

"Oh, tomorrow evening most assuredly. Would you like to leave a message?"

A slight chill reached up Susan's back. All pleasantries now? Why the sudden change of heart? And then an even more sickening thought entered her mind, a thought she hoped was nothing more than her vivid imagination.

Hope

Susan dialed her mother's cell phone. There was no answer. The day following, it was all she could do to take in the tasks at *Honesty House*. Jane had known something was wrong, Susan had seen it in the girl's eyes, though she seemed happy that a decision had been made. Both girls, one twenty-five, the other, twenty-nine, would be starting work on Monday.

Susan had finally found Oscar alone. She'd walked over to him in the main room to speak with him. He'd glared when he saw her. She'd sat down anyway.

"How are you doing?"

"Fine," the boy responded.

"Did you miss me?" she'd asked.

"Were you gone?"

Susan remembered her heart breaking in that moment. "I just wanted to talk with you for a minute or two."

"Times ticking."

She'd reached for him but he'd recoiled. "I don't know what you expect," he'd said under his breath. "You leave for two months and then return here as if nothing has changed. Well, everything has."

Susan had looked at the full tables, the children, many of them playing games, laughing and talking. This room, nor the rooms that some of the children lived in, at least until their parents got things together, would ever be quiet again. And it was a good thing, a dream realized. Except now, now that she wanted to talk to Oscar privately, he appeared angry—and the place was suddenly much too noisy.

"What's changed?" she'd asked, trying not to yell over the children.

"You. My sister. Jane. My mother."

"I heard about that."

"He killed her, you know."

"Who killed her?"

"My Father."

"But your father is already dead."

"I know, but he still killed her. She tried everything to get better I know she did."

Susan reflected briefly on the trauma of previous years, even before the *Hotel Camaro* and the lone children that hung out in the front yard, mud stuck between their fingernails, dirty clothes and hair. They'd smiled even then, as if making mud pies was the greatest sport on earth. And maybe it was. It was definitely the only thing that had remained constant then.

And now?

"You know I love you," she'd said.

"You got married. You left us."

"I'm sorry about that."

He'd looked up, tears welling in his eyes, though he'd brushed them away quickly. "I have to take care of Brianne. We can't count on you."

The words were still hurtful, but the boy was obviously in pain.

"What about Jane?" she'd asked.

"I don't know."

"Didn't she take care of you while I was gone? You still had a place to stay, a place to eat, to sleep when you needed it."

"We didn't have you," he'd said and the tears had begun to multiply once again.

Susan had thought her heart would break. The child was obviously upset and well he should have been. She had left for two months and during that time his mother had died and he'd taken on the extra burden of caring for his sister. Sure, he'd a place to stay, a place to eat, but that hadn't been enough—couldn't have been enough.

"Well, I'm here now," she'd said, wrapping an arm around his shoulders. This time Oscar had taken her gesture in. "I will never leave you again. Sure, I'm married, but the time will come when you and your sister will be able to come and live with Henry and I. Would you like that?"

She hadn't meant to speak of the adoption so soon; it would be months before everything would be finalized, but the time had felt right. The boy was thirteen after all and he needed a bit of stability to carry him through. The future would be that stability.

***

The return call from her mother came the morning of the following day. "So, Kate is here. William said she's seeing some beau."

"That's right." Susan's heart thundered in her chest. Her mother was alright! Thoughts of her lying dead somewhere, poisoned by the wicked William, filled her mind once again, but only briefly this time.

"William said you were pretty insistent about seeing me. I was at the spa."

"Oh."

"A gift from William. 'A bit of pampering is what you need,' he said and then he handed me a gift certificate to the *Blooming Palace*."

"Oh."

"Is that all you can say, daughter? It was magnificent. A royal spa with every imaginable offering. I should take you sometime."

"That's okay."

"So you don't want to go."

Her mother was amazing. She read between the lines like some pro editor. It was just like her to feel her disinterest in going to a spa, just like her to hate her because of it.

"If you want, but I really..."

"So what did you want to speak to me about?" Hope asked. Susan held the cell phone to her ear, but her hand was not steady and she wondered if her voice would give her away. She never expected her mother to call and that was wrong, but William had been so secretive about her whereabouts she'd been almost certain that something unnatural had happened to her. What was worse, she hadn't planned on what to say.

"I...I..." she stammered, "I'm worried about you," she said, wishing in that moment that she hadn't said a thing.

"Whatever for?" her mother asked plainly.

Susan's thoughts tumbled. *Why was she worried?*

"Well, you got married too, without even talking to me and I'm not so sure about William." There, she had said it, though until saying it, she hadn't been completely sure how she felt.

"Dear, sweet William? I can hardly believe it. You'll just need to get to know him, that's all. He speaks highly of you."

"Really?"

"Yes...*really*. What was it he said when you talked to him at the door?" Hope paused. The line was silent. Finally, she breathed, "It was something about your interest in knowing where I was. Your *insistency*, I think he said. Told me he liked that in women."

Susan was bothered by the comment but she tried to respond as politely as possible.

"That's nice."

"Nice? Praise would be a better word. Told me he didn't want to give out the information on my whereabouts because we'd discussed that it should be a secret. He did say, however, that you had a surprise visitor with you. So, when did Kate get in? I'd like to speak with her."

Kate blinked at her from the couch and did some sort of quiet sign. "She's gone back home," Susan lied.

"Are you sure? That would hardly make her stay a week."

"Ah, something happened at work and she had to get back."

"That's too bad. So why did she come to see you?"

"To apologize, I think." Susan looked over at her sister who was grinning at her. This conversation was unbelievable. How would she be able to keep her sister's visit a secret? Why had she said that Kate had returned home?

"Serves her right," was her mother's reply. "You two never got along well. So why couldn't she call?"

Susan shrugged though her mother couldn't see it. Kate continued to smile at her from the couch.

"Kate...she felt terrible about treating me so bad after Bob's death."

"Well, she was pretty stiff. Sorry," her mother added lamely. Perhaps she was thinking about Bob's rigor mortise after death. Susan might have laughed if this whole situation was anything but funny. "Did you have a nice visit?" she asked.

"Oh, sure." Susan peered over at her sister who was taking another sip of Pepsi. "We had a great time—ah, short as it was."

"That's good. So how would you feel about coming to dinner?"

"Dinner?" Susan squeaked.

"Well, naturally. You need to get to know William better, so you're not afraid of him."

"I didn't say..."

"Can you come? And you can bring Henry, of course."

Calm?

The serving of food would come sooner than later. Her mother was always prompt, always perfect, always so pleasant. She looked over at William. He sat at the head of the table, his grin matching the bright yellow shirt he wore. Henry sat next to her. Occasionally he would touch her hand and her heart would calm.

She'd left Kate alone at the house. After another few days of less than pleasantries, Susan was ready for her sister to return home. But the word had finally gotten out. She *had* left her boyfriend and was needing some consolation. But not only that. Her job was on the rocks, had been ever since the funeral, after her return and some of her fellow employees had ganged up on her to weasel her out.

Susan couldn't believe it. Kate was broke.

Her mother smiled as the casserole dish was laid out on the table. The asparagus was already in the decorative dish, followed by rolls and a green salad. "Let's get started," her mother said, sitting down and brushing something invisible off her flowered apron.

Susan bowed her head to pray. But the room was as silent as the grave.

"There's no need for that," William offered, scooping up a plateful of the casserole and passing the dish to Henry. "I'm atheist."

Susan looked over at her mother. She had suddenly paled.

"Oh," was all Susan was able to manage. She felt a slight squeeze of her hand and reached for the asparagus with the other.

After the meal, everyone gathered in the living room to continue the bland conversation that had begun at dinner. She'd hardly said a word and had heard very little. William was atheist? The thought of one among them not believing in God filled Susan's mind with dread. Her mother wasn't perfect in the sense of being a true Christian, but she had always taught Susan the basics of doing unto others and sharing what one had—even if it wasn't much. For all the terror her mother sometimes provided, from strange ideas to even stranger mood swings, there was one thing Susan had always been able to count on from her mother and that one thing was prayer at supper.

How had her strong-willed mother found William in the first place? How could she have stuck by a man who was as far away from her own belief system as the sun was from planet earth?

She might have cried if she hadn't been so shocked. And now they were sitting in her mother's white on white living room as if everything was alright. But it wasn't alright.

"So, tell me about *Honesty House*," William asked, crossing his legs and peering over at her and Henry, though he'd rarely looked at Henry the entire time they'd been there. "I hear it's quite the fixer-upper now."

"Oh, well, the place is for children now and..."

William laughed. "How do you keep the drug dealers out?" he asked.

"Drug dealers? Well, it's no longer a hotel. I... well, there were two children, are two children that I care about very deeply. I guess that's where it all began."

"After the bad guys were all put in prison I take it," William said.

Susan's heard thundered. She had no idea where the strange questions were coming from, though she wondered if what Henry had recently told her about William's jail time had something to do with his line of questioning now. Her mother sat next to her 'beloved' silently, as if he was merely talking about ice cream with fudge topping. Susan wondered what Henry was thinking. Would he interrupt this strange conversation, take it in a different direction, ask William one of the questions weighing heavily on her mind? Probably not. He wouldn't step in like that, expecting her to shift the grief if she chose to. But how could she?

"Everyone is in jail." She stopped there, wondering what to say and then it was just time to say it. "So where did you two meet?" she asked, her hands perspiring, though it was a simple enough question.

William laughed. "Not in jail," he offered. Her mother laughed, though the comment wasn't funny—at least not to her or Henry.

"We met at the supermarket," Hope said. "I was craving some lobster and there he was, standing next to me on the other side of the tank."

"I tried to keep my claws in," William said, "but your mother was so beautiful, the thought of holding back was difficult."

Sudden humor? Where was this coming from? Susan glanced over at Henry. He squeezed her hand again, prompting her to continue.

"How long did you date before marrying?"

Hope smiled. "Just two weeks. I could hardly wait."

She sounded like a teenage girl talking about her new boyfriend. Just two weeks?

"What day?"

"The 25th."

"Of last month?"

"Of course, daughter, what did you think? I'm not a spring chicken anymore and William, well, he was a great find."

William smiled over at her. "Your mother is a great cook and a great lover."

Susan was embarrassed. She dared not look at Henry. "Oh," she croaked.

Hope sighed. "You should probably keep some of the facts of our marriage a bit more private," she offered, but her voice was quiet.

William stood. "Well, that was nice," he said, walking to the kitchen. "Anyone up for a drink?"

***

"Don't you think he's a bit—odd?" Susan asked. Kate watched in anticipation. Despite the fact that Henry had learned a few things about William from his desk job at the precinct that she didn't care to repeat—twice as a teen he'd been jailed for ripping off a convenience store and just five years ago he'd been released from jail the third time for another robbery—this one with a threat to the employee's life. She still considered the man odd with or without the jail time.

Still, she tried to imagine a man her mother's age trying to swipe the little money that could be had at a gas station till, a black ski mask across his face, but it was no use. The sight of it just made her laugh, though she had to admit that the idea did feel a little creepy.

"Who is odd?" Kate asked.

"You should have seen William at dinner," Henry began, sitting down on a chair opposite the couch and peering over at her. "Remember how he treated you at the door?"

"A bit rough around the edges," Kate said.

"Well, he did the same thing at dinner," Susan said, sitting down on the couch by her sister. "He was funny with Mother—the things he said weren't right."

"Like what?"

Susan explained about him being atheist, how she hadn't been allowed to pray and the fact that the man had been so blatant about he and his mother's sex life.

"Is that all?" Kate asked, though she seemed a bit unnerved at her comments.

"Is that all?" Susan repeated.

"Well, yeah. Many people are atheists and many more probably share more about their sex life than they should."

"But it was the way he said it." Susan looked directly into her sister's eyes. "And the way he looked at Mother. She was afraid of him."

"Now you're getting at something," Kate said.

"Do you know that Mother and William had only been dating a few days when he proposed and she accepted?"

"How long?"

"Two...weeks."

Susan thought of the man, Matthew, her mother had been dating seriously during the *Scrambled* case.

"Whatever happened to that guy Mother was dating a couple of years ago?" she couldn't help asking.

"Oh, he flew the coop right after the Christmas party."

"Well, it's not like that hasn't happened before." Susan stood, wiping her palms down her worn but still sufficient Levi's.

"But this bit about her being afraid of William, why do you think that is?" Kate asked.

"Maybe because he's been in jail a few times," Susan answered.

Kate jumped. "Why didn't you tell me this before?"

Susan swallowed. Her sister was angry, but the anger would just have to wait. "Because..." She paused, searching for the right words, "...we didn't want you to worry. Isn't it bad enough that you've lost your job and that you're secretly hiding yourself here to discover the murderer of Bob..."

"I can't believe it! Don't throw that stuff at me!" She glared over at Henry, though she, herself, had been the one to say the last words.

"Look, we're sorry."

"Sorry? Sorry! Why do you think I'm here anyway?"

To get a free ride, Susan thought but didn't say. Her sister was broke and with no job and no prospects, she had to live somewhere. If not at the home of their crazy mother and no boyfriend to speak of, where else could she go?

***

"I'm sorry. I'm just frustrated, that's all."

She had talked to Henry, spoken with him until he was blue in the face, but he'd never said 'I'm sorry,' no, not once. And now, here she was talking to her sister, the woman who never apologized for anything.

"I know I'm wrecking things with you and your husband," she continued, turning to the window and looking out.

It was definitely November with its blurring of yellows and oranges, and in its place colder air and damp streets. Susan couldn't help it. She loved her sister and wanted to help but wondered if Kate was right after all. Was her sister disturbing the connection she'd once had with Henry?

Kate turned. "I'm so sorry, Susan."

Was that tears in her eyes?

Susan stood from the bed and wrapped her sister in her arms. "It's okay, really," she said, wondering if today, like most days recently, the skies would be clear, the air peaceful though a bit chilly.

Henry had left the house angry and she didn't care, at least that's what she told herself. But standing here, next to her sister, she wondered. "Henry will get over it," she said, pulling herself from the hug her sister still had her in and looking into the woman's eyes. "And it's not your fault."

"I think it is. You're in the honeymoon stage, after all."

Susan laughed. "YOU don't believe that corny stuff, do you?"

"I didn't used to. But when you love someone, all sorts of terrible things can happen when someone horns in like me."

Was Kate horning in?

"I promise to do better. Besides," she said, walking to the mirror and taking a second look at herself. "Perhaps I'll find the killer after all."

A slight chill raced up Susan's back as she looked at her perfectly attired sister.

"In the meantime, I can look for work and maybe find a place for myself nearby—to give you and Henry some more space."

"That's not..."

"Oh, but it is," Kate returned, turning from the mirror. "I'll get a job, help you solve the murder of your ex—and do it all without Mom even knowing I'm here. If Henry can keep feeding us both information and you can keep prodding Mom for whatever else she may be hiding, I'll do a bit more of my own sleuthing. I'll find the killer, you can bet on that."

Susan was not a betting woman, but she hoped her sister was right.

Confession

"I guess I shouldn't have told her," Henry said as he dressed for bed. "But she is living here, after all and she is helping us solve the murder of your ex, though I'm really not sure why."

"She loves me, that's why."

"I know that." Henry reached for her hand. She didn't take it. "What I meant was, her love for you can't be the only reason she is searching for Bob's killer."

"She has nowhere to live, doesn't have a job." Fortunately, for both of their sakes, Kate had decided to go out for the evening. That left a free house and no one listening in at the door.

"I know that too. Really, Susan, hear me out."

She stood like molten rock, but her heart was pounding mercilessly in her chest. Was this what marriage was like? Always second guessing the other person?

He pointed to the bed. She sat and he followed. She hadn't yet dressed for bed—didn't want to until this whole tirade had been resolved.

"I did some checking. On your sister." He paused. When she said nothing, he continued: "I just felt like I had to know if there was anything we should be concerned about. There was."

"You're kidding."

"I wouldn't kid about something like this."

"What did she do, smoke pot as a teenager?"

"Actually, yes," said Henry, squirming a bit on the bed. "But that wasn't the only thing in her file."

Susan's heart stopped. What could her sister possibly have done? She had had a good job, had lived on her own for years. Had had a perfect life until recently.

"So what did she do?"

Henry touched her hand. This time she didn't remove it, but allowed the warmth to enter her heart. Henry would always love her, no matter how much they fought.

"Forgery."

"Forgery?"

"Evidently it happened a few years ago. She's lived secretly in New Jersey ever since."

"You mean, here?"

"That high corporate job you thought she had at Jenkins Fidelity, well, she hasn't worked there in five years."

"What?"

"She's been here, working as a waitress, trying to clean up her life, I guess."

Susan was dumbfounded. It was impossible!

"Until recently, she was still on probation."

"How long was she in jail?"

"Two years."

Susan recalled the less than comfortable visit where she'd been jailed for only a short time when the police had discovered the 'planted' gun in the secret place behind her bed. She remembered the surprising $100,000 in bail money her sister had paid so that she could leave that horrid place. How had her sister come up with the money if she no longer had her old job by then and was working as a waitress?

"I don't get it. My sister bailed me out of jail, remember?"

"I remember."

"Where did the $100,000 in bail money come from then?"

"I've thought about that," Henry offered. "Wouldn't she know people with money, maybe an old boyfriend—someone who might help her out?"

"Could be. Especially if that boyfriend was still seeing her when she came to see me. Are you going to tell her or am I?"

Henry stood. "I'm not sure. I'm not even supposed to be looking at this stuff at work unless I'm assigned. Everyone at the precinct and beyond still say it's suicide. No one's looking into anything and I have to hide what I'm doing from the boss."

"Oh." It suddenly occurred to Susan what a risk her husband was taking, hiding his searching like he was and she wondered what might happen if he got caught. Still, the risk was necessary, wasn't it? Didn't she need to know what had really happened to her ex-husband?

It was funny, but if she hadn't known Bob so well she would have believed the reality of the suicide, even with the note like everyone else. But Bob had taken painstaking care to follow her when she left him. He'd even gone so far as to pay Frank Olmstead, the unlucky jewelry salesman, to see what she was doing. It wasn't like him to give up—no, not even if he couldn't have her.

Sure, he'd lost interest in work for the most part and had become some sort of lounge potato, but he would never end his life because life wasn't working out the way he wanted it. He would have just continued forward until he got her back, or found some other woman as an unlikely substitute. The idea created chills up and down Susan's spine, but it was the truth. Bob wouldn't ever give up—for anybody.

"I'm sorry about earlier," Susan said, reaching into the bottom dresser drawer for her pajamas. "You're right. Kate has every right to know. She's living here after all and helping us along. Wouldn't it be funny if she really did find my ex's killer?"

***

Jane was in an uproar. The new girls, Miranda and Chelsea, were about as thick skinned as the tree out front that still hadn't been trimmed by the gardener.

Susan tried to smile. "Where are Oscar and Brianne?" she asked.

"In the kitchen. The dears offered to help with lunch. Where have you been?"

"Sorry," Susan offered truthfully. "We've had quite the family stuff going on the last couple of days and it looks like things are not going to get better soon.

"That's too bad," said Jane. She smoothed down the flowered apron over her slim bosom. "I am missing you something fierce. I thought when you returned from your honeymoon things would get back to normal."

"Sorry." Even as she repeated the words, Susan knew that even one-hundred sorry's would never be able to rectify the stress and worry that Jane continued to have even though she'd returned. "I'll do better."

"That's good. It's about time I had a week off."

The words were sudden. Susan looked into Jane's eyes and could see pain there and this time it wasn't as hidden as in previous days since her return. Would she be able to run *Honesty House* without Jane? But looking at her now—seeing her tired eyes and listless posture, there was only one thing that she could do. The new girls had been hired and, evidently Oscar and Brianne had become part of the family—at least part of the *Honesty House* family. Could she say *no* to this friend who had supported her these last few months?

"It's settled then. Time for your own vacation."

"Really?" The words flowed from Jane's mouth like water. "I mean, I know you need me but..."

"But nothing. You deserve this time away. How does two weeks' sound?"

"Heavenly!" A gush of emotion filled her face. "Are you sure?"

"I've never been so sure. And I want you to start now."

"Now?"

"Pack your bags. Things will be great here and when you return, you will be refreshed to help me do a little more remodeling."

Jane smiled. "Are we actually going to add on the play room?" she asked, her eyes searching the corner where the wall would be removed and the room expanded for play.

"Yep. It's about time we make this place more than a room and board establishment."

"Although it's more than that," Jane said, standing. "Much more."

***

Two days later, Susan was wishing Jane back. But she was visiting with her parents in California, a long-awaited trip that had finally—and with very little thought—come to fruition. As much as the children helped and Miranda and Chelsea did more than their fair share, *Honesty House* was still a burden in so many ways.

There were children to feed, get to sleep, to keep busy doing things that wouldn't get them into trouble. There were parents to deal with—parents who either didn't understand the program, or felt as if *Honesty House* was taking away their children. These same parents couldn't hold jobs, drank to excess, did drugs, left their children at home, alone, unattended for hours and frankly, often forgot they had children in the first place in favor of satisfying their own needs.

In the midst, there were the few good but poor parents who did their best, but their best wasn't enough so *Honesty House* would pitch in. Near dinner time, when even the stragglers had finally settled in—there were only so many beds and some children would have to be turned away—Susan would collapse on the couch and remember Henry. He would be waiting for her yet again, the meal (recently re-heated) on the table. With droopy eyes, he'd be waiting for her, whether she returned home at 8, 9 or 10 p.m.

Both Miranda and Chelsea had been hired as live-in caretakers and would stay the night with the children, but Susan would be expected to return early the next morning, to take over the morning shift.

Henry was sleeping on the table when she walked in, a not so hot bowl of soup sitting in front of him. His red hair was no longer parted but fell across his left cheek. She stood there for a moment watching him, remembering the first time she'd laid eyes on him; the first time she'd seen his apartment with the resin chairs. She'd loved him even then although she hadn't known it.

Walking to his quiet form she touched him lovingly on the head. "It's time to eat," she said, but he didn't move, though she could hear him snoring slightly. "Henry!" she said louder, stroking his red hair, trying to part it like she'd first seen it, like the entrails of a fish.

His head bobbed. "What?" he asked.

"I'm home."

"Oh. I must have fallen asleep." He wiped his lip. "Let me re-heat that for you."

She sat, looking down at the broth. "It's perfect," she said, placing her pinky finger inside the liquid.

He nodded. "Mind if I go to bed?"

She smiled over at him and followed him down the hall to the bedroom.

***

Kate was still yelling. "Do you mean to tell me that you've known all about me for weeks and haven't said a word?!"

"We wanted to make sure we had all of the facts before talking to you," Henry said. He was pacing again. He always paced when things got just a bit out-of-hand.

"I should have known you'd search me out. You're a cop after all."

"Thanks," Henry said. He stood up straighter.

"It wasn't meant as a compliment."

Susan searched her sister's eyes but saw nothing but anger brimming over. Was she angry about the truth coming out, or was there something else going on?

"Look, you two, I've almost got enough money to move out. *Rich's Delicatessen* has hired me back on, though it took endless begging on my part to get my job back."

"You didn't steal from them I hope."

"No, I'm a forger, remember?"

"Same thing."

Henry couldn't have been blunter if he'd slapped Kate in the face.

"I don't see you as Mr. Perfection," Kate said, striding into the kitchen. "I need a drink."

"Get one for me, too?" Susan asked, though she'd meant to keep quiet. This conversation wasn't going to be an easy one—for any of them.

The drinks poured, Kate returned. "Here," she said, shoving a glass at her. "For your information, I was 'let go' because I was having a difficult time getting to work on time."

"You're kidding."

Kate looked down at her glass and took a sip. And then another. "I probably shouldn't be doing this," she said.

"Why not?" Henry asked, though Susan could see that he was still in his higher-than-thou attitude. "You've been living here for four weeks now. Our house is your house..."

"I'm pregnant."

No one spoke. A minute or two ticked by. "Are you sure?"

"Sure enough, sis. Near two months at my last count."

"Why didn't you tell us?"

"Probably for the same reason you didn't discuss my sordid past—until now." She placed the empty glass on the coffee table. "So, now what do we do?"

Susan had no idea. The bomb had landed. In the midst of getting fired from a job she loved because of a greater love of forgery, going to jail because of her crime and in the process getting pregnant and losing her boyfriend, her sister had come here—here of all places. And Susan had no idea what she was going to do.

***

The following morning, work came early for Susan. She remembered and not with fondness, all of the things she'd learned from her sister the previous night.

Not only had Kate's boyfriend left her soon after the probation period had ended, she'd discovered that she was pregnant. He was gone and she wouldn't tell him—couldn't tell him.

She'd decided to keep the baby, there was no way she could abort and yet as the baby had grown inside her, so had her insecurities of what was to come. She couldn't raise this child alone and she couldn't go home to Mother. But she could go home to Susan.

Susan thought of contacting her mother with the news. It would relieve some of the burden, but in the end and with the helpful tears of her sister, she and Henry had decided against it. Kate would remain with them, at least until the baby was born.

"So, what do you think of my pancakes?" Oscar asked, the griddle still warm from serving.

"Terrific. You're getting to be quite the cook."

"That's what Jane says. When did you say she'll be back?"

"In a week and a half."

"Oh, right."

Susan looked down at Brianne who was clearing up the breakfast dishes at *Honesty House*. Some of the children helped, but she always took it upon herself to see that everything was completely cleared. "What game are we playing today?" she asked.

"Not sure, but you'd better hurry. School doesn't wait."

Brianne looked up at her but she wasn't smiling. "I hate school," she said. "I'd rather be here."

"Well, you'll be here until kingdom come if you don't go to school and get some education."

"I'd rather be here," Brianne said. She placed the last container of syrup on the table. "I need to wipe this mess."

"I'll do that. You and your brother get off to school."

Oscar tugged at his sister's sleeve. "The boss has spoken," he said. Susan reflected on the paperwork that still hadn't been finished for the adoption. The children, for all intents and purposes were at another foster home until everything could be sorted out, though they still spent much of their time at *Honesty House.*

***

"I know you're keeping her with you!" Hope screamed into the phone.

It was all Susan could do to remain calm. So, William had finally opened his big, fat mouth. "Sorry, Mother."

"Why is she there?" The screech was insistent, though her mother had toned down some. "Why hasn't she called?"

Kate had already left for work. It was near 11 a.m. and *Rich's* would be opening for lunch.

"She didn't want me to."

"Why not?"

"Because she didn't."

"That isn't like Kate."

Susan's hands were visibly shaking. Since the discovery of Kate's recent past, Henry had also dug up a bit more on her mother's secretive husband. Evidently, the man was still being watched. Though Henry wasn't completely sure why, the records pointed to possible money laundering. Susan wondered if her mother knew about it and if so, how she'd managed to work through the knowledge along with thoughts of being married to an atheist.

"Susan?"

Susan realized her mind had drifted. "Sorry, Mom, what were you saying?"

"I'm here for a visit. Are you going to answer your door?"

"Where?"

"At your house."

"I'm at work."

"I'm at your house, and it's cold out."

"Sorry, but I'm at work."

"Unbelievable! Why are you at work?"

Susan looked around her. She hadn't had time to tell her mother that she was anywhere, what with her flying off of the handle about Kate. Why had she gone to her house without calling first?

"I'll be there in twenty."

"Twenty minutes? By then I'll be a frozen popsicle!"

"It's the best I can do."

"Then forget it."

"Sorry."

"Sorry! Is that all I get for trudging all this way for nothing? The least you can do is offer me and your father some dinner tonight."

"What?"

"Dinner. You do still cook dinner. I need to speak with you—and your sister. We'll come by tonight, say around 6:30, and talk."

***

Near 6:30, when her mother and William were due to arrive, the air was crisp in more ways than one. Kate had returned from work, having worked the early afternoon shift and she was all frowns.

"I can't believe you told her," she said. "I'll never hear the end of it."

"I didn't tell her. It was William."

Kate sat. She'd already removed her filthy apron and had changed her clothes—into one of those ensembles that had initially made Susan think Kate still worked at Jenkins Fidelity. "And perhaps there's a way to share the information and allow William to relax enough to share a tidbit or two about his life."

"More than we already know?" Susan asked.

"Of course. I have some questions for him as I'm sure you do."

"Like what?" Kate asked.

Henry looked over at the clock on the wall. "We only have a few moments and your mother is prompt. Perhaps she doesn't know that her beloved was once in jail. And what about the two weeks they were together before getting ma—"

A knock on the door shortened Henry's words. Susan got up from the couch. "I'll get it," she said. It was 6:30 on the nose.

Kate blinked at her as she passed and she wondered how afraid her sister really was. How much would her sister reveal and how much would William fess up to? Time would tell.

She opened the door. Her mother was alone. "Where's William?" she asked.

"I don't know," came the reply. "I just don't know."

Susan opened the door for her mother to enter. The tears that had begun had suddenly halted when she saw Kate. "So it's true," she said. "You really have been hiding out from me."

Kate stood and embraced her mother, something Susan always had a difficult time doing, but for some reason, Kate managed. "I'm sorry, Mother," she said. "I just wanted you to be proud of me."

"Proud of you? I've always been proud of you."

"I'm pregnant," Kate offered.

Susan's eyes turned to her mother, but her mother was revealing anything—at least not now.

The dinner was a success. Either that or everyone liked the lasagna from scratch that she'd cooked up. Very little was said and it was up to Susan, it seemed, to keep the conversation going. Unfortunately, there was only so much one could speak about when it came to the weather. Finally, when dessert was being served— chocolate cake with fudge icing and a lather of ice cream, Hope spoke up.

"So you're pregnant. What other secrets are you keeping from me?"

Susan could see Kate visibly swallow. She dabbed her lips with a napkin and said, "I've lost my job."

"Your job at Jenkins?"

"Yes." Kate took a bite of cake."

"And what about your boyfriend, the one I've never met, is he taking any responsibility?"

"He doesn't know."

"Doesn't—"

"Look. I'm doing my best. Susan and Henry were gracious enough take me in."

"What else haven't you told me?"

Kate laid her fork down. Her face reddened and it was all Susan could do to remain silent. She loved her mother, but in the same breath, she knew how difficult it was to get through all the mud and muck that always seemed to make its appearance when she was in the room. "Perhaps we should be asking you the same thing about William."

Hope stopped chewing. She swallowed and standing up, excused herself.

Susan watched the back of her mother's head as she left the room and walked down the hall to the bathroom.

"Well?" Henry whispered. "What do we do now?"

"I have no idea. You're the cop. What would you suggest?"

Henry's face paled. "Maybe you should go after her."

"How about Susan? She has a way with Mother."

"What?" Susan gaped, trying to keep her voice down.

"Like I said. As hard as your mother is, she seems to listen better when you speak."

"That's because she hates me," Susan whispered.

"She doesn't hate you," Kate began. "You have just done all of the things she wished she could do but has never had the courage to do. Why do you think she married William?" Her hand went up suddenly over her red lips.

"Maybe you should tell me," Susan said, her heart was pounding, but for some reason she really didn't want to hear the answer.

"Well, Susan, you got married. Just met the guy—sorry, Henry. Why wouldn't she feel like doing the same thing?"

"Mother wouldn't have done anything like me—that just doesn't make any sense."

"Well, maybe she was tired of being alone."

As Susan drew in some air to speak, Hope returned, dabbing at her eyes with a tissue. "Tell her," Kate said suddenly.

Susan blinked.

"Tell her what?" Hope sniffed.

"What you told me, while Susan was on her honeymoon."

Hope sat on the nearest chair and peered over at her. "Bob and William knew each other. I found out after our marriage. He told me how surprised he was that Bob was in the family—well, you know. After you married Henry, William seemed to ease up a bit where Bob was concerned, but it was like watching a cat and a mouse sometimes."

Susan sat in her own chair and stared blankly at her mother.

"William told me that he and Bob were friends and that they'd worked together. Except, Bob had swindled him out of some money, so ever since then they hadn't spoken. That is, until the day I brought him home to meet the family. He told me later that he almost didn't marry me because of Bob and then thought better of it."

Something was not right here. And it was looking more and more like William may just have done it—killed her ex as a way of getting back at him for swindling him. Still, it was a large price to pay, your life.

"So, how much did he take?" Henry asked.

Hope blinked. "I don't know really. Just know that it was quite a tidy sum."

"Which makes me wonder why William went to jail but never Bob," Susan said.

"What?" Hope croaked.

"I mean, I'm sorry, Mother. We should have told you. William should have told you."

Kate wiped her slim hands against her jeans, probably feeling relieved the topic of conversation had turned. But Susan wasn't so sure the misdirected conversation was for the best. It was like a swarm of bees had infested the living room and before long, they would all need some healing ointment.

***

"Kate, you'll come with me." It was a statement rather than a question and Susan wondered how her sister would handle it. They had spent over three hours in that living room, talking about William and Bob and her involvement, until the conversation had finally travelled her sister's way.

"So, your beau left you, you're pregnant, you lost your job...what else do you need to tell me?"

Kate winced but remained silent. Finally, she said, "Nothing, Mother. That's it."

But as Susan watched her eyes, she knew that something was missing in the mix and that thing was the job at *Rich's Delicatessen*— perhaps, if her mother got lucky, that tiny bit of information that had gotten her there in the first place would be revealed.

"You'd better tell her, she'll find out anyway," Susan said suddenly.

"I work at *Rich's Delicatessen*," Kate said, staring away at nothing.

"That greasy place?" her mother offered. "Why?"

"It was the only place I could get a job. After..."

"After?"

"After being in jail."

Hidden Answers

Her mother was furious. After the last revelation, she had been happy to leave Kate alone. Through tears that Susan rarely saw coming from her sister, her mother had not relented. She was "done" with Kate, or so it seemed. She had messed up her life, it was up to her to fix it.

The door shut, everyone but Kate breathed a sigh of relief.

"She hates me."

"She doesn't hate you." Henry got up. "She couldn't hate you, you're her daughter." He'd pronounced the word *daughter* slowly, probably not wanting Kate to miss the point.

Anger could never really out rule love; in time her mother would mellow, Susan thought to herself. She would accept Kate once again into her life. It was the way things went with her hard-boiled family. Forgiveness would come. It would have to come. But what of her mother and her atheist husband? What a cruel turn of fate that had brought them together! God couldn't be a part of this mix, could he? Two people, so terribly different could never be led to one another by God, or could they?

The questions still remained. Why had her mother married after only two weeks of dating? Why would a man be interested in marrying after just a few short weeks? Could a man be civil one moment and dangerous the next? What did Bob have to do with any of this? Was he in the wrong place at the wrong time, or was he part of the problem?

***

Susan took Brianne and Oscar aside. Evidently, the two had gotten themselves mixed up in a problem of their own.

"She lied to me," Oscar said.

"I did not," Brianne pouted. "You've got to believe me. He started it."

"I did not."

"Did too."

"Did not."

"Stop." Susan raised her hand like some sort of street cop. "You two have got to learn to get along. You will be with each other for a few years yet..."

"Until I'm eighteen," Oscar said, glaring over at his sister. "And get away from her and—this place."

"Why?" Susan asked, so sure that *Honesty House* was the best place either of them could be in.

"The place is cramped and you're always taking in kids like...like stray cats, that's why."

"Oh." Susan wasn't sure what to say. Was Oscar just angry, or did he really feel this way about *Honesty House* and what they did here? But his next words surprised her even more.

"I'm ready for a real family," he said. "No more of this fake stuff."

"You're fake," chimed his sister, poking him briefly in the stomach. "Fake, fake, fake!"

"I am not! At least I tell Susan the truth! Unlike you, you liar!"

They were at each other's throats again and Susan, plain and simple, had no idea what to do. And then it came to her. A simple answer, one her mother might have even been proud of. "Tell you what," she said, looking down the hall to the kitchen. "What would you think if we fixed our own meal tonight and ate alone outside by that big tree—all by ourselves, while the other kids ate inside?"

Brianne blinked. "Do you really mean it?" she asked.

"Is this some kind of trick?" Oscar queried, peering even closer into her eyes. "I'm not taking any more lies."

"No lies." Susan raised her hand again. "Just good food."

***

The meal was revealing. At least here, bundled for warmth under the large oak, she could learn something about the children that would soon be inhabiting her own home. She'd gotten permission of course, from the foster care mother, but getting permission was easy—far more difficult was keeping the kids for all time.

But it wouldn't be long now.

Until then, she would do what she could to ease the stress the children were facing.

"When will Henry be coming around?" Brianne asked.

"You miss him?"

"Of course, though not as much as you." The remark from Oscar was candid. There was no question that he could use a father and she would go downtown this very week to see if the paperwork could be rushed.

"How was your honeymoon?" Brianne asked. "I know you must have kissed, but I also heard that you caught a killer. Was the captain of the ship really the bad guy?" This time Brianne looked at her deeply waiting for an answer.

"Yes, he was really the bad guy."

"I don't think I'll ever go on a cruise," Brianne continued while her brother chewed on the fried chicken they'd placed on plates for themselves. "With people dying and getting poisoned and stuff, we could be next."

"No. I doubt it. Most times people have a wonderful time taking their cruise and they don't get hurt or killed or anything."

"Really?" Brianne's light brown hair was pulled into a pony tail today, her eyes wide. "I think I would be worried anyways," she said.

"Anyway," her brother corrected. "Besides, Susan isn't a real detective. She just helps out, right?"

"Right." A small chill raced up her back, a chill she didn't like.

"Susan doesn't have a badge or drive a police car. People just like to die whenever she's around."

Susan might have laughed at that, though the comment from Oscar held some truth. People were known to die around her, even if not right next to where she was standing. Since leaving Bob she'd become a death magnet she was sure of it. Why else would she return home only to find her ex husband—dead? Well, at least she hadn't been blamed this time around.

"I think I'd like to be a detective some day," said Brianne now, taking her first bite of chicken. "I think it would be fun..."

"Fun, ha! You just said..."

Susan tried to shoo the comment away like a huge fly, but the boy continued, "People go on cruises all the time and you can't be afraid to go on one if you're a detective."

"Is he right?" Brianne asked.

"I'm afraid so. As a detective, you have to be open to going anywhere you might be afraid to go, especially if you think that criminal activity is lurking there."

"*Lurking*, what's that?" asked Brianne, taking another bite of chicken.

"Something mysterious happening. You can't be afraid of anything mysterious because you never know when you'll discover a clue."

Susan thought briefly of the past few days. How had she felt talking with her mother? How did she feel about talking to William? Could she talk to him without anyone else around, or would her fear of the unknown keep her from doing her own detective work?

***

"I've come to talk," Susan said, sitting once again on the white couch her mother had recently cleaned after the death of her ex.

William sat across from her. They were alone. She didn't like it that they were alone, but she was glad of it nonetheless. Now she could ask him anything.

"I have some concerns about..." No, that was the wrong way to begin. He'd just get defensive. "So, where's Mother?"

"Shopping, for a new outfit."

"I'm glad I caught you then. You do an awful lot together." She smiled over at him and wondered if William could tell her smile was pasted on—fake.

When he smiled back in a similar way she was pretty sure of it. "You know, Susan, I may not have told your mother everything about me, but she knows everything that really matters." He brushed a hand over his bald head.

"Like what?" she asked.

"That I love her, for one. That she makes me happy and that my life is finally and completely the way I want it."

"But you know what a past does," Susan said, trying not to leave his eyes. "It makes a person what they are today. Sometimes...it even follows them."

William coughed, once and placed a hand on either side of his knees. He was wearing dress pants and a navy sweater over a white shirt. "And sometimes it doesn't."

"So what attracted you to Mom?"

He hesitated for only a moment. "Her good looks, the way she took care of herself, her love for God."

"What?"

"Surprised? Well, knowing and loving God makes or breaks a person. In your mother's case, it made her who she is."

"And you?"

"I don't have any room for God and unfortunately, he has no room for me."

"How do you know that?"

"You're the one who brought up the past. And perhaps you're right. The past is hitting me square in the head at exactly this moment. Thank you, Susan."

Susan was suddenly more uncomfortable than she'd been when entering her mother's home and finding that he was alone. He'd let her in, though she'd preferred to stand at the front door and talk. He'd been somewhat civil, almost friendly and so she'd relented to his request to come inside.

"There is talk..."

"You shouldn't believe everything you hear. I don't."

"There is talk that you were once in jail." There, she'd said it.

"Sure, when I was a kid. I'm not a kid anymore."

"But what about the stuff with Bob?"

"You mean, your Bob? Oh, excuse me. What used to be your Bob?"

A chill raced up Susan's back. The shield was falling and she was pretty sure she would see William sitting there in all of his true colors in just moments.

"Yes, Bob. He took my money, on a sort of...business venture."

"What, may I ask, was the venture?"

"Sold me a home that wasn't his."

"Bob?"

"I had a lot of cash at the time and he was working with another fellow, a Mr. Olmster, I think it was."

"Frank...Olmstead?" she gasped. Her heart was gone, or so it seemed. Frank, the unlucky jewelry salesman who had stayed at the *Hotel Camaro*, was suddenly making a surprise appearance.

And then another thought came to her.

"How could my ex and this Frank Olmstead have swindled you out of money?"

"You didn't know? Well, of course not."

"Know what?"

William stood and walked to the window. "Your ex—was quite the conniver. "I thought he was a bit brainless, too. But he wasn't what he appeared."

Well, Bob was Bob and he couldn't fool her. There was no way Bob could have fooled an ant into following him. "How did he get you to invest in the house?"

"He showed it to me. Up on the hill. Empty. Had the key and everything. I paid him cash, only to return the following week to find people already living in it."

"Who?"

"I don't remember, but the house was in Nevada; a beautiful little place in a godforsaken part of the world. It was a quiet place and sat all alone by itself. It's just what I needed at the time." He paused and continued to look out the window. "Had a difficult time getting back on my feet after my name was attached to various burglaries around town." He turned, smiling.

"But I'd cleaned up my act—that is, until your...Bob swindled me out of all that money. There was no paperwork drawn up, nothing to prove that Bob had done anything wrong. And I was left holding the empty bag so to speak."

"So you killed him. A fine revenge."

She hadn't meant to say it, at least not so soon, but there it was, on the tip of her tongue and flying out of her mouth like a rabid monkey. When would she learn to curb her words?

"Killed, Bob?" He seemed momentarily surprised and then relaxing his facial features he returned to his chair. "I can see why you'd say that. I did have a motive, if you will."

"And?"

"And I didn't do it. I didn't kill Bob."

"What were you doing in the shed with the antifreeze just hours before his death?"

William's head jerked up. "What?"

"The antifreeze in the shed. Kate saw you with it."

"She did, did she?"

"And that's just one of the two mixtures that the police found in Bob's drink."

William stood again. "I think it's time for you to go," he said. "Your mother will be home soon."

Susan looked down at her cell phone. It was near 3 p.m. "And then what?" she asked. "Will you tell her what we've talked about?"

"You mean what you've accused me of. No, Susan, I won't say a word. We are living in the present, remember?"

Susan stood, leaving her glass on the end table in which she'd never sipped. Not even once. But she'd been sitting on the white couch after all and it had been William who had poured the drink.

***

Jane was all smiles. Two weeks later, she'd returned as promised, all aglow with tales of meeting a fine man. But, she relented, it was time for her to return to work. Work made her feel fulfilled, it encouraged her and made her feel as if she was making a difference in the world. And she wanted to make a difference.

Susan was so happy to see her. So happy she embraced her and squealed.

Jane was appalled. "What?" she gasped, trying to release herself.

"Things haven't been the same without you," Susan breathed. "Not the same at all!"

Jane laughed. "You're kidding," she said, pulling herself away. "You really missed me that much?"

"We missed you," Brianne said. Oscar nodded.

"Well, what do you know. I missed you all, too." She squeezed each of the children in turn and turned as Ms. Pratt approached. "The kitchen has been a living terror."

Susan gulped. The woman hadn't spent but two seconds in there since Jane had left. But she didn't say anything, better not to say anything and stir things up. She'd talk to Ms. Pratt separately, square her on the way things should have been when Jane was away. And then another thought occurred to her. Why hadn't she fixed this kitchen problem before Jane's return?

She hadn't been the same since her return from the Hawaiian Islands. And now with Kate still living with them and the children soon to inhabit their home, it was all Susan could do but put two feet in front of the other. Had she lost her touch? What had happened to her dream?

Looking over at Jane she wondered, if, through all the slips and turmoil of the cruise, she'd slackened her grip on things relating to the *Hotel Camaro* now *Honesty House*. She wondered for the first time if the place was no longer hers—emotionally speaking, that is—if she'd already left it in the hands of one, Jane Dove, without even realizing it.

***

"If I have to wait on another table or cook when the chef gets sick, I'll just die!" Kate wailed, plunking herself down on the couch.

Susan watched her sister from the kitchen and it was all she could do but keep her tone even and in control.

"Maybe you can look for a better job."

"Don't think so. I'll be as big as a house soon."

Susan thought of the house they were living in and how quickly it would be crowded. Was Kate planning on living here even after the baby was born? No, she said she planned on moving out—but when would that be, she wondered. It would have to be before the children came to live with her and Henry.

"Can you stir this for a moment? I need to talk to my husband."

Kate walked into the kitchen and reached for the spoon. "I'm sorry," she said. "I should be of bigger help to you. You are taking care of me after all."

"Just stir the sauce," Susan said, leaving her. She traveled down the hall to the bedroom. "Honey?" she asked. He was sitting at the computer, their only computer, attempting the bills. He looked up.

"We need to talk." She closed the door.

He turned.

"The kids, they are asking for more time with you. They miss you."

Henry blinked. "I know. I need them, too. How much longer?"

"Just a few more weeks. How long do you think it will be before Kate leaves?"

He shrugged. "How am I supposed to know? Have you asked her?"

"I guess I need to."

"Why don't you ask her now. I'll be a few more minutes." He turned.

"But what about the children?" she asked.

"I'll stop by tomorrow on my lunch hour. I could do with a little less paperwork."

***

"I've quit my job," Kate said. "Maybe after the baby..."

Susan was furious. "The baby? I thought you were moving out..."

"How can I? What will I do with a baby? How will I pay the bills?"

Susan blinked. She stared at her sister. Unbelievable. Her sister was unbelievable. "What am I supposed to do?"

"How am I supposed to know. Do you know anything about raising kids?"

"What do you think?"

"Well, you must have learned something taking care of Brianne and Oscar."

Susan rolled her eyes. "I never watched them as babies."

"Oh."

"Besides..." She sat by her sister on the couch. It was past time to go to work; Jane would be livid if she took much longer. "They will be coming to live with us soon. I just don't know if I can handle two children plus you, plus a baby."

"Oh. I never thought of that."

"Seriously?" She hadn't meant to say it but there it was. Her sister's face was streaked with tears and she was still in her pajamas. A small mound where her flat stomach used to be filled out her pajama bottoms. She would need maternity clothes soon and with no job and no money coming in, she'd never leave them. And she needed to leave them. This was *her* time. She and Henry's time. She and the children's time. And then an obvious thought came to her.

"We are having some difficulty with the new cook," Susan began, eyeing her sister closely for a hint of understanding. "The woman is having a difficult time staying focused on the tasks at hand. Even the children have had to pitch in just to make sure that a meal is served."

"That would be a problem. A place needs a steady cook with a good head on her shoulders, one who can manage the food."

"That's why you'd be perfect for the job."

"Me?"

"Of course."

"But I primarily served at Rich's. I did very little cooking."

"But you know how to cook."

"Of course, though the smells are starting to get to me. Like hamburger, for one."

Susan took a deep breath before proceeding. If her sister worked at *Honesty House,* cooking and serving them, perhaps she could save up enough money to move out and take care of her baby. She had no idea what they were going to do for a babysitter, but the answer would come in time. With everyone putting their heads together, things would work out.

"How would you feel about working as a cook at *Honesty House?*"

"Your place?" She seemed visibly shocked. Henry was already at his desk job, so the time couldn't have been more perfect. She could only guess what he might think.

"You can start in two weeks. I have to give some warning to Ms. Pratt."

Kate smiled. "You're too much," she said, her face softening. She reached over for a hug, planting a kiss on Susan's cheek. "Too much!"

***

"I found it behind the couch," her mother said, displaying a piece of paper in her hand. She held it like poison, like somehow, the paper might reach out with its 'non hands' and bite her. Susan read:

Dear Susan,

I can't Believe you're married. With my Love still brimming over, I Thought, Somehow, that you'd still be Mine. You are MINE, aren't you, Susan? I don't know if I can Survive without You. But I will Survive. I will go on. Maybe I will find someone as you have.

bob.

Susan looked up. The paper had been balled and then opened, obviously, by her mother.

A slight tear entered Susan's left eye. "I think," she answered, "it means that Bob definitely did not commit suicide.

"Maybe this was the first try. He threw it behind the couch before making a second attempt with the suicide note."

"But I don't think the other note is a suicide note. I think someone planted the note to make it appear a suicide." Susan eyed her mother closely. "The first note...it wasn't dated, was it? And weren't the pen colors different? Red and black?" She squinted her forehead trying to remember: "The paper was different, too."

"What does that matter? You should have seen him the last few days before you arrived home, before Kate came to support the family because of his death. He had no family members to speak of if you remember—no mother or father to come to his funeral. But, of course, they were there in spirit."

"Of course," Susan mumbled, trying hard to keep the words against her mother's new husband tucked inside.

"That man moped around like his life had ended. William and I tried to pull him out of it, to no avail. He went out little, did little for himself in those last days. I told the police how depressed he was."

"You did what?"

"Told them the truth. They asked me, Susan. They stood right over there by the kitchen—I'd fixed them a drink—and told me that the note coupled with what I and William had shared with them made perfect sense. A week later, they were handing me back the suicide note."

"They didn't ask around? What about Bob's old friends? What about that sneaky Mr. Olmstead?"

"Who?"

"He was one of Bob's friends. Went to jail. Should be out by now, he was sentenced for only two years."

Her mother brushed a slim hand through her gray, red hair. "He never said a word about that man." Susan thought briefly of Frank Olmstead, the man who'd swindled thousands with his imitation jewelry he'd sold as the real thing. And she couldn't help but remember his spying methods for her curious husband and more recently, that he'd been working with Bob to swindle William. What could the man be doing now?

"What about your husband?" If Susan had thought ahead, the question would never have come spilling out, but as it was the words had come right out in the open.

"My husband?"

"Well, yeah. How well do you know him, really?"

Her mother blushed and sat down her drink. "I was wrong to have called you," she said. "Wrong to have told you about the note."

"Why?"

"You know why. It's always been the same with you, Susan. Blaming me for your sorry life."

Susan could hardly think straight. And was that? Her heart trying to leap out of her skin?

"I don't blame you for anything, Mother."

"You blame me for pushing you to marry Bob."

"What?"

"Just what I said. You blame me. You think I pushed you into him and so you went out and divorced him and shacked up with that no-good Henry, just to get me back. Well, at least you came to your senses and married him."

Thoughts of pain whirled through Susan's mind like a volcano with liquid red lava. "What?! I married Bob because I wanted to. You had nothing to do with it."

"But I helped you two meet, I coaxed Bob in the art of dating, I pretty much married you off..."

This was the first-time Susan had heard anything about the coaxing, though she remembered that her mother had introduced them. It was funny somehow, like the Queen of England introducing some squire. "When did you help Bob with dating?"

"He was real shy and because I knew him pretty well and you, of course, I instructed him on what to say."

"You didn't."

"I did and let me tell you his charm worked wonders on you. I remember you coming to me and saying, 'Bob is perfect. He knows me and loves me for who I am.' I almost blushed and maybe I did as you told me about your undying love for the man I had trained to be just the sort of husband you'd want."

For some reason, the sound of her mother's words made Susan sick. She had 'trained' him? For what? To be some sort of soldier boy, some sort of perfect man for her? Is that why the next few years had felt so odd with him? Why he'd gained so much weight, why he'd seemed to change as the years wore on? But that was true of all couples, wasn't it? Didn't everyone grow and either the couple grew together or apart?

"I tutored him, Susan. For days, when you were at work or somewhere else, he'd come here and I'd tell him what to say. I thought in time he would get it on his own, be able to talk with you the way you needed and wanted."

Susan was sick. She couldn't believe it. She couldn't believe what her mother had done. Was her mother so sick, or so controlling that she'd had to control the very man she was doomed to marry? Now everything made sense. The change of attitude. The change of apparel. The inner change, like something different was there that she'd never been able to put a finger on. Bob had been friends with Frank Olmstead and the man she now knew as William. Who had Bob been, really?

Last Stand

Honesty House was closed up for the night and Susan wiped a weary hand across her eyes. She was dead tired, but more than that, she had no idea how she was going to reconcile her feelings of betrayal with her mother. They had left one another in speaking terms, though her mother had to know that her heart had not healed from the inflicted abuse—probably would never heal.

Her marriage had been a sham. It had been as fake as the days were long. And her mother had been part of the pain. Everything. The long nights crying because she couldn't have a child. The days with Bob when he hadn't wanted to go to work—though maybe something illegal had been happening right under her very nose when she went to her job.

She had not yet spoken with Henry and she wasn't sure how she'd be able to, not until her eyes stopped welling with tears and she felt as if her next breath wouldn't be her last. Telling Henry, filling him in on the details of her mother's delusion would fill her heart again with pain and Henry's with anger, she was sure.

But the time came, as it always does, when something presses on your heart. Kate was asleep in the room down the hall and she and Henry had some time to be alone—and talk. Only he wasn't listening and in moments, as she spoke to him about the pain of her heart she could hear him snoring beside her.

"Henry!" she whispered as loudly as she dared.

"W-what?" He blinked, opening his eyes.

"I'm trying to talk to you about my mother and all you can do is—sleep?"

"Sorry, honey." He yawned. "Tell me again."

She wanted to get angry but instead brushed his thick, red hair. "Tomorrow. We can talk about it tomorrow."

***

A week passed before Susan again received the strength to talk to Henry about her mother. She'd already given him the news of Kate, which, amazingly, hadn't sent him into a rage. Interestingly enough, he thought it was a good idea. "She needs a good job and you need some time away," he'd said.

And now he was finally listening in as she spoke to him about her mother's lie.

"Wow," he finally said when she was finished. "I knew your mother with a little 'off' but I had no idea she'd do something like that."

"For all the good it did..."

"It makes one wonder if that's one of the reasons your sister was adamant about not going to your mother's place. It's okay for her to stay here, for now, but what about in the future?"

"I've thought long and hard about that one too," she said, patting the bed next to her. "Her baby won't hold itself in just because Kate doesn't have a place to live. And with the children coming..."

Just then, as if on cue, her husband's cell phone rang. As Susan stared at him his face lit up. "Ah-huh. And we don't have any more paperwork? And the kids... This week? Sure. We can make it work."

***

"The police aren't too concerned about the second note," said Henry, dropping his lunch bag on the counter. "Another love note," they called it. One of the cops even winked at me. "Sorry, honey."

"Doesn't surprise me."

Kate looked on from the kitchen sink where she was rinsing out Susan's favorite mug. Susan had just told her the news and her sister had taken it quite well, though there was sadness in her eyes.

With November here, coats and leggings had suddenly become mandatory. The children coming to *Honesty House*, for all intents and purposes, had little to keep them warm, though donations arrived sporadically. And in just two days the children, her children, would be here.

Court proceedings would occur tomorrow and the children would be theirs.

Most of her thoughts now concerned getting the rooms ready for her children. It was upon cleaning the corner of her sister's room—they'd finally found her a place to stay at *Honesty House*—that Susan had found the note. It jolted her like a million thunderclaps as she stood there in the room that was soon to become Brianne's quiet place, holding the crisp piece of paper.

Dear Kate, the words read in heavy printed ink. *I don't know how much longer I can survive with this woman. I miss you. I miss our time together. Love, William.*

***

"Henry!" Susan bawled into the phone. "You have got to get home. Now!"

"Susan, what's wrong. The children..."

"The children are fine. It's about Kate."

"What is it?"

Susan's hands shook. She couldn't even believe she was saying it, let alone thinking it. But it had to be true. William was Kate's ex-boyfriend—old and bald William, with the perfectly pressed pants and steely gray eyes.

"Come home!" She pressed the cell phone to the off position and sat wearily on the couch. What did this mean, exactly? Why would William marry her mother when he obviously loved Kate? Was the baby his child? And why hadn't Kate said anything about knowing him? She acted as if they'd just met. What sort of ruse had the two of them cooked up? And what did the ruse have to do with her ex-husband's death?

She sat for about twenty minutes before the door opened. Henry rushed in. "What is it?" he breathed. "I must have gone through three red lights just to get here. What is it?"

"You'd better sit down."

Henry plunked himself down in a chair opposite the couch. He didn't ask for any explanation, but waited for the moment she would tell him.

Susan stood, handing him the newly pressed note. She watched as Henry's eyes scanned the document. And then, he looked up. "I can't believe it," he said. "Why would an old man like William care one red cent about your young sister?"

"Besides the obvious reason?"

Henry blushed.

"Because *he* got her pregnant, that's why."

"What?" Henry stood, pacing the living room. "Do you think they knew each other at Jenkin's Fidelity?" Henry brushed a hand against his forehead and then his fingers found his hair. "This little bit of news should strike up some questions at headquarters."

Susan held her breath. Along with all of the new thoughts she had about William and her sister, another thought floated within her brain like a flying trapeze-man.

"I don't think we should. They think we're both jokes as usual, right?"

Henry paled.

"Well, at least I'm the jokester like normal," she added quickly, hoping not to have offended him. "I think it's about time we took this case on. Ourselves."

Henry walked to the couch and sat down next to her. "What do you think this juicy bit of news means for Bob?"

"All I can figure is that Bob was living in his in-law's house, which one day became his ex-in-law's house. If Kate and William were seeing one another and if William is the father of her child, he took off, not wanting the responsibility. He traveled here, met and married your mother—quickly—and just as quickly your ex is killed and Kate must make her journey here to attend the funeral. Only, maybe she didn't come because of the funeral. Maybe she came for another reason."

"What could the two of them be cooking up?" Henry asked.

"I have no idea. But don't you find it strange that everything is connecting like some crazed puzzle? Bob and William knew each other. And Kate and William obviously know each other. The bottom line? The dial keeps pointing to William."

***

Kate was no worse for wear, though she looked tired. She was quiet, too, and would only speak to Susan when spoken to.

The day wore on and by evening, when Kate was signing out, Susan made it a point to talk to her. Jane Dove had been busy the entire day keeping things in order and she was away again, probably in the rooms. The groundskeeper, Mr. Gobel, had already left them and fortunately, she no longer had to worry about Ms. Pratt. Her sister was doing nicely.

They sat. Her sister was in a shining green top with straight leg jeans and a semi-high heeled shoe. Some things never changed, though the look in her sister's eyes now was anything but pleasant.

"I feel like I'm going to throw up," she said. "I thought it was just morning sickness, not morning, afternoon and evening sickness."

Susan looked up at the clock. The time was 3:30. Brianne and Oscar would be returning home from school at any minute and by the weekend, they would both be living with her. She had to act fast. Honestly, it had taken her the entire day to drum up the courage to speak to her sister. She'd gone through the words she would say a million times, at least. And now there was no more waiting.

"Tell me about William," she began, trying to calm her heart by taking even breaths.

"William?"

"Yes, William. You know him."

"Of course I know him. You're crazy. *You* know him."

"I mean, tell me about before. Is he the father of your child?"

Susan took a deep breath and held it for only a moment, though her head began to spin as she expelled the air and her sister looked at her—suddenly—as if she'd seen a ghost.

"W-what?" she stumbled.

"You heard me. News is, you knew William even before Mom did."

"Who told you?"

"So, I'm right."

"Of course you're right!" She stood, her silver heels clomping against the flooring. "I mean, I knew him. We—we worked together."

"At Jenkins?"

"Yes."

The answer was barely a whisper and when her sister turned, large tears were streaming down her sister's cheeks. "I made a mistake."

"So, the baby is his?"

Her sister nodded. "He left me, you know. Left me high and dry when he found out. I looked for him, even. I was stupid."

"And Mom? Does she know?"

"Of course not." Her slim fingers reached through her brown hair. "He followed me out here, after everything. Left his own job to be with me. He waited until I was released—after I'd spent some time in jail. I think now he only felt guilty because I'd been caught and he hadn't."

"And the pregnancy?"

"That's the funny part," her sister said, sitting next to her on the couch and wiping a hand under her eyes. "Have a tissue?"

Susan reached into her purse.

Kate blew her nose and continued: "We were only friends at first. But as time went on, I guess I kind of grew—attached."

Susan would have laughed out loud if her sister hadn't sounded so serious. She watched her sister's eyes, the way they'd look intently at her one moment and the next, away, very far away, before returning. She wondered what it all meant.

"So, you knew William had married Mother."

"That's the other funny part." She sniffed and blew her nose again. "I came for your ex-husband's funeral and was shocked out of my gourd when I saw William standing next to Mother. Can you believe he only smiled at me?"

"Have you talked to him?"

Only briefly. Just once actually. He avoids me like the plague. That day I saw him in the garage with the anti-freeze, I asked him about it and his once warm eyes turned to me—they were like ice, as if we'd never really known each other. He said, "So, what are you going to do now, Kate dear. With the baby, I mean?"

I wasn't sure what to say. Do. I reached for the anti-freeze. He hadn't expected that. I pulled it from his perfect fingers and began to unscrew the lid. Suddenly, you could smell the stuff like ripening fruit. But I hadn't been quick enough. In moments William had the container back and was re-screwing the lid back on.

"What do you think you're doing?" he screamed at me. "Trying to kill me?"

"Of course!" I yelled back. But I would have said anything—then, I was so angry. He'd left me and the baby and had gotten married to someone else!"

"And not just anyone," said Susan, imagining for a moment how she'd feel. But she'd never been in a situation like her sister, for all of the bad fruits and rotten escapes she'd had to make in her own life. What could she possibly say now?

And then Susan remembered the note. She pulled the piece of paper from her purse and handed it to Kate. Her sister scanned the note briefly, then looked up, her eyes no longer shining with tears. What Susan saw instead was anger.

"Where did you get this?" she wailed.

"In the room. I guess you thought you'd disposed of it."

"Ok, so I... still love him and he loves me. Does that surprise you?"

"Why did he marry Mother?"

"He won't tell me."

"That's funny," said Susan.

"Look, I don't expect -" In that moment Brianne and Oscar came into the room. Susan could hear them even before she saw them.

"Just two more days," Oscar said.

"Two!" Brianne squealed. "Is the room ready yet?"

"Almost." Susan turned to her sister. She was wiping frantically at her tears.

"So, maybe it's almost time to celebrate," said Kate, offering a hand to the two. "This calls for a party, don't you think?"

Brianne jumped. "Do you mean it, Auntie? Can we have a party?"

"Well, if it's all right with your future—mother." She smiled, but in the smile Susan could see something hidden, as if riding low within, until the appropriate time came for whatever it was to be released.

***

"Kate admitted everything. The child is William's. And they're still in love. It's unbelievable, but Kate has no idea why he married my mother."

"So, should we tell her what we know?"

"I don't know. I've been worried about that the entire night. And something else."

Henry turned to her, placing his arm under her head. "People in your family. I have no idea what to think."

"Why do you think I stayed away for so long? They're crazy if you ask me. I'm worried about Kate and the baby and I'm worried about Mom. If she finds out...but she must find out. Her husband is keeping secrets."

"Though I'm not sure you should be the one to share the information," Henry offered. "I mean, shouldn't it be her husband, or Kate?"

"I have a funny feeling growing in the pit of my stomach. I'm not sure what to do—all I know is that I can't live with things being so hidden as they are. Something needs to be said, by someone. I don't know how much longer Kate can hold out. She has a lot on her plate. And besides, she told me not to say anything and I agreed."

"Why?"

The sorrowful look in Henry's eyes made Susan turn away for only a moment. "Oh, I don't know. Maybe because I love her and want her to be happy." The words stung at her eyes. She wiped them briefly with her hand. "Kate was always so perfect, so everything. And now...I don't know how she'll make it if I say something to Mom."

"Maybe something should be said to William."

Susan turned to her beloved. He would always be her beloved no matter what they went through together—because, in reality, everything from here on out would be experienced—together.

"I don't know. What if he gets angry?"

"He might. That's why I want to do it," Henry said, taking her hand. "Maybe we'll learn something at the same time."

Susan smiled but she didn't feel like smiling. Something ached inside her, burned almost, as if the fire that was growing would never be extinguished.

The Truth

"I can't believe it! We're finally here!" Brianne sang.

Oscar stood silently nearby surveying the living room and kitchen. "Looks okay," he said.

"Okay? Boys are dumb," said an eager Brianne racing down the hall. "Where's my room?"

"The first door on the left," Henry said.

"Where's mine?" Oscar asked.

"On the other side, to the right, just past the bathroom."

"Figures," he said, walking to the room. Susan and Henry followed, saying nothing. This would be an adjustment for both of them, though Brianne seemed to be taking the change swimmingly.

"So, what do you think?" she asked, looking inside, hoping that the little girl, now her own, liked it.

"Oh, it's beau-utiful!" the little girl sang again, twirling in the yellow room like some mini-dancer. "How did you know I liked yellow?"

"You told me."

Breanne smiled. "Oh," she said. "Where did you get the fluffy pillows?"

Susan looked down at the yellow striped pillows on the girl's bed. "IKEA," she said. "Do you like them?"

"I love them!" She reached for one now and pressed it to her. "And the closet! It's so big!"

"I'm glad you think so," said Henry. "I didn't do anything but paint it."

"And put these cute stickers on it, I bet."

Susan had almost opted out of the yellow smiley faces, that could be removed, surely, if the girl didn't like them, but Henry had been insistent. "She's needed a bit of happiness for a long while," he'd told her.

Well, at least in this case, he'd been right.

"I'll have plenty of room for my shoes—when I get them," Brianne added airily, turning to face them both. "I'm hoping to get all of the colors."

"I didn't know you liked shoes," Susan said.

"Oh, I love them! Only, I haven't been able to buy them—until now."

"You have a job then?"

The girl smiled. "No, but you do. I can have some new shoes, can't I?"

Susan's heart skipped a beat. She turned to Henry. "Of course you can have some new shoes," she said, "only not all at once."

Brianne beamed. "That's okay," she said, plunking herself on her bed. It was white with a yellow ruffle on the sham. "I've waited such a long time for a mother and father—" She hesitated and looked out the window as if seeing someone. "I never saw father much and mother, well you know how she was. I'm just glad to have some real parents."

It was a kind gesture, but more than that, thought Susan. The girl's eyes were intent and searching, her light brown hair combed to the side with a barrette. For just an instant Susan thought of the first time they'd met, across the street from the *Hotel Camaro* now *Honesty House* and the way she'd looked then, all grimy and dirty, her hair caked with mud, her clothes covered in filth. She remembered the house, more like a shanty. "Perhaps we should see how Oscar is doing," she said.

Susan reached for Brianne and gave her a tight squeeze. Henry did the same in turn and in moments they were making their way to Oscar's room. He was sitting on the bed, large, wet tears dripping down his cheeks. He wiped them quickly as they approached.

"You're not my real mother," he said.

"I know."

The boy sat on the bed and fidgeted with the comforter, a dark blue, matching his mood. So, she'd probably picked the right color for his room too.

Henry sat. "I know I'm not your real father, either," he added, "but I hope to be able to help you have one terrific life."

"How can you do that?" the boy asked. He looked up now, meeting the eyes of Henry.

"Well, you have this room. It's all yours. Your...Susan will expect you to clean it, of course, but this will be your responsibility."

The boy frowned.

"And," Henry added, when the boy continued to sulk. "We are going to do fun things as a family."

"Like what?"

"Well, what do you like to do?"

"Play ball."

"Baseball?"

"Yeah, but I never had a mitt. And balls were hard to get unless you stole one and kept it hidden from prying eyes."

Susan blinked. Had the boy really had nothing then? They'd kept plenty of play paraphernalia at *Honesty House*, including bats and balls. But maybe the boy wasn't speaking of that. Maybe he wanted his own set.

"My dad once played ball with me," he said, "before the drinking started and he started to hit—it was Mother mostly. When he'd come for me I'd hide or go outside and make mud balls for protection. I only used them once."

"What happened?" Henry asked, wrapping his arm around the boy. The boy winced, slightly, but didn't brush her husband's arm off.

"He came for me. I hit him square in the face. He swore and then..." The boy sobbed then, placing his hands across his eyes and wiping them in a continuous motion of grief and pain. He reached for Henry and clung to him. Susan could hardly take it in.

Oscar cried for some time and when the crying eased, Susan went to him. "I tell you what," she said, kneeling in front of him. "We'll go and get you a brand-new bat and ball..."

"And a mitt," her husband finished. "You can't play real ball without a mitt."

"Do you mean it, really?" Oscar asked, lifting his head from her husband's shoulder and staring into Susan's eyes.

"Of course. We'll go tomorrow."

"Tomorrow," Henry echoed.

***

"Have you seen Kate?" Hope wailed into the phone.

"Sure, she was at work today." Susan thought of the way her sister had looked when she'd come downstairs from her room at *Honesty House* this morning—half her former self, or so it seemed. She reflected on their day together before she'd left suddenly for the evening. "Maybe she's just—out—she is a grown woman, you know."

"A few minutes ago, she called and then just hung up. I tried calling her back with no answer."

"She's out as far as I know. Left about eight."

"Why would she call and just hang up?"

"I don't know. Mom... please."

"I'm worried. Where are you now?"

"Home."

"Can you run over there and check up on her?"

"Sorry. Kids are finally asleep. Henry's asleep. I can't leave."

"Aren't you worried?"

"No, Mother. Kate's fine."

When her mother was no longer on the other end of the phone, Susan reflected on what she'd seen in Kate's eyes that very day. Returning to her own room she dressed for bed. Henry was already asleep, his hair flopped to one side like the entrails of a large fish. How she loved him.

***

Kate was gone and Jane had no idea where she was. Everything was gone; her clothes, her toiletries. When she didn't show up for her cooking assignment Jane had gone up to find the room empty.

Susan was worried, but her sister was a grown woman after all. She obviously hadn't liked the room situation, but what other alternative had she and Henry had?

Jane Dove was frantic without Kate. And now, as always, Susan was getting the brunt of Jane's worries. "I need her! You come in so sparingly now. I understand, don't get me wrong, it's just..."

Susan listened to her long-time friend and she knew something else, knew it as distinctly as if a sign hovered over her friend's head.

Finally, the words came but not from Susan's lips.

"I'm sorry. I should be more concerned about your missing sister than I am about my own hide."

Susan blinked. A small tear fell to her cheek. *Where was her sister?* Surely, her mother, having found her, hadn't dragged her to her house. The thought of it made Susan sick. Well, if her sister was there, perhaps some important things had finally been talked through.

***

Susan sat across the table from Jane. It was early afternoon and a few children hovered within the area playing board games. She would have to speak softly.

"I don't know how to tell you this, but..."

"You're leaving me, too," Jane said, leaning in and taking Susan's hands. "I knew it."

"How?"

"You haven't been the same since you returned with Henry." She smiled, a slight tear running down her left cheek. "Do you think I'm stupid or something?"

"Not stupid. Smart. That's why I want you to take over the business. Hire whomever you need. I will be here until you do. I don't want to leave this place but Oscar and Brianne, they need a mother now. I just can't farm them off to a stranger."

"I know." The words were tender. Another tear entered the woman's eye and fell down her cheek. "I can find who I need. As for *Honesty House*, honestly, I'm not sure I can do it without you."

"You're kidding, right? You took charge during my honeymoon and after."

"I know, but owning a business. I've never done that before."

"And I've never been a mother before."

Jane smiled. "I do have some money set aside..."

"When you're ready, let me know. For now, what I need is someone to manage the place. You'll be doing what you've already been doing and I'll increase your pay until you can buy me out."

"Thank you."

"Well, then, it's yours. What do you think of that?"

"I think..." and here Jane paused. "I think you're the most generous person I know."

***

After three days of searching, Kate still hadn't returned to *Honesty House*. She hadn't returned to work and she hadn't been seen by her mother. Jane had hired a perfectly fine cook—a Mrs. Grimble. Older surely, but with enough spunk to knock your socks off. Jane said she was perfect for the children and she agreed. Jane would do fine.

Though only a few days had passed, Susan had grown more than a little worried. *Where was her sister*? The woman, for all intents and purposes had simply—vanished.

There had been no help from William, little help from the police. William was either a complete stone or a lying fool, but the man had been firm in his opinion. Kate had probably taken off somewhere. Wasn't the girl 'flighty' after all?

The police 'were looking' they said, but had found nothing yet.

The truth of William and Kate remained a closed book, but two weeks later, with no word from her sister and a mother crazed with worry, it was time to confront William.

They were at her mother's and William stood before them like a burning match.

"You what?" he hollered, taking Susan by the arm. "You think, what?!"

"I think you killed her, that's what I think!"

"Let go of my wife's arm!" Henry screamed. Taking William by the shoulder, William released his grip.

"You have the nerve coming in here and threatening me like that! I'm calling the police!"

"Yes—please! And they'll put you in handcuffs!"

Hope looked visibly shaken as she entered the room.

William forced a smile when he looked at her mother, at least it seemed forced to Susan whose heart was beating like a thousand drums. "It's alright my dearest. We'll just take this conversation elsewhere so you can get some rest."

"You will not," Hope said.

William flinched. "Honey, just go back into the bedroom, I'll join you soon."

"W-what is going on?"

"I think she has a right to hear this," said Susan. "It does have to do with her."

Hope reached for William's arm. "What has to do with me?" she asked.

"Nothing."

He wrenched himself free. "I will not speak of this with *her* here."

"Then we'll tell Mom what she needs to hear without you here." Henry reached for William and drew him away.

"Tell your wife about the baby."

Hope paled.

"I said, tell your wife," Henry prodded.

"It's not mine I tell you. Kate is lying."

Hope released her hand. "What are you saying?"

"Kate's baby, it's William's," Susan offered.

"What?" The woman stared blankly at her husband. She hadn't yet combed her hair although it was noon. She was still wearing her silk pajamas.

"I tell you, Hope, it's not true."

"Kate is pregnant with *your* child?"

William was silent. He looked angrily into Susan's eyes and sat down, offering his wife a chair next to him. She didn't take it.

"I tell you, the child is not mine. I know...your daughter. We worked together at Jenkins Fidelity."

"Then you *are* the father."

William blanched and gave Susan another hateful stare. "I knew her because we worked together. We were both fired because..."

Susan blinked. Now, he would share it all...

"...of the forgery scam."

"Forgery?" Hope glared down at him, her eyes shooting bullets.

"Just here me out, darling. I've known your daughter for some time, but that doesn't mean I'm the father of her child."

"Can you prove you are not the father?" Susan asked.

"Of course I can. Kate, she's just angry with me."

"For what?"

Now William stood and walked to the window. It was perhaps a minute or two before he spoke. Susan wondered what he might say. Do. More important, she wondered what they would all learn so that they might once and for all learn the location of her sister.

"She is in love with me."

Hope walked to William. The man she thought she knew. The man who'd betrayed her. It was all in her eyes, in her body language as she stood before her husband.

"You're telling me..." she cried, "that Kate *loves* you?"

"She wanted me, but I wouldn't give in. Even after..."

"After what?"

"Telling me she was pregnant. She said she needed a father for her child. I told her I was too old for her, we'd never...anyway, I didn't love her. At least not in that way." The man turned, his eyes burning. "You need to believe me. I didn't touch her, not once."

"Then whose baby is she carrying?"

"Not mine."

"Why would she tell me then that you're the father?"

"Like I said, she loves me."

"According to the note I read, you love her as well."

"What note?"

"The one you wrote swearing your undying love to her."

William turned away. "I had to do that," he said. "It was the only way to get her off my back."

"You wrote Kate a *love* note?" Her mother was visibly shaken.

"I find it strange that you married our mother knowing how Kate feels about you," Susan said.

"I had no idea my wife was Kate's mother. We had a simple wedding, didn't invite any of the children...If I'd known..."

Hope's eyes whirled with fresh tears. They cascaded down her cheeks and fell to the top of her pajamas. "You wouldn't have married me, is that it?"

"That's it. Though you need to know I love you, Hope."

The man stood at the window, his wife of only a few short months staring at him. Her eyes did not soften even after he'd left the room.

***

"I've left *Honesty House*."

"You what?"

After a less than leisurely visit at her mother's, a visit that had turned even more sour when her mother had commanded them to vacate it, she had finally and with reservation, decided to drop another bomb.

"I know it will mean less money coming in, but Henry, I've just got to be here with the children."

Henry's eyes softened. He walked to her and they embraced. "I know, I know. I have wondered the same thing. So, you didn't find anyone to watch after them during the day?"

"I tried, but the point is, Henry, I need to be home with the children, whether I'd been able to find someone for them or not. Jane will do a fine job. She's going to manage the business now and later, buy it."

"Are you sure that's what you want?"

Susan turned to the hall. Brianne had entered it and was staring up at both of them. "Are you ready to watch the movie?" she asked.

***

"I'm worried that something has happened to her," Susan said, pacing the living room where Bob had been murdered. Unfortunately, they knew little more than the basics when it came to his death, the police department positive that he'd killed himself.

Still, as Susan walked, or rather, paced the living room along with her mother; William had left her, she wondered if her mother would ever be the same again. It was amazing that she'd let them in. It was amazing that she was talking to them now. What was even stranger? She was still in the same red pajamas from days previous. Yet, for all her mother's strangeness, her pet-peeves about cleanliness, her ranting and wailing about how William had sorely disappointed her, Susan still loved her.

"What if he doesn't come back?" Hope asked.

"Maybe that would be for the best," Susan answered assuredly, sure of one thing. Her mother couldn't do any worse living alone if William decided not to come back. Had he told them the complete truth? Or had he played the game with Kate only to discover that she wouldn't return the favor. Could he be protecting his own hide? Could he in actuality be the father of Kate's child?

Two stories, both differed. Whom should she believe?

"It's been three weeks! I have checked everywhere here that I can think of. And you..." Hope began.

"We've done some of our own checking. Nothing," Henry said.

"What of the police?" Hope asked.

"They say the trail is dry. Not even William's past has given them the answers they need." She caught herself before she said more. He'd robbed a convenience store when he was nineteen and had spent five years in jail for 2nd degree robbery with a firearm—so he knew how to use a gun. He'd also threatened bodily harm to the employee at the gas station, so he'd probably have it within him to threaten Kate into doing whatever he wanted.

And yet, Kate and William's stories didn't match.

William had also known Bob and suddenly it occurred to Susan that Bob more than likely had had some contact with her sister—maybe even while she was in jail.

"Where did William say he was when Kate went missing?"

"Well, let's see if I can remember. She didn't come home that night but William was with me, at least for the majority of the night. I told that to the police and they checked William's whereabouts when he wasn't with me. Appears he was at the club."

Susan breathed in. She was getting nowhere with her mother and her mother appeared a bit agitated.

"Did you check her previous place of employment, *Rich's Delicatessen*?"

"Yes, mother."

"And the police, did they talk to Jane, that woman who works with you at *Honesty House*?"

"Her too."

"What about the children, they must know *something*."

"Kid gloves on that one, Mother. They asked, but only as they could ask children."

"Right."

"So where do you think she is?" Susan asked.

"What about the others she worked with at Jenkins?"

"It's been awhile. Some of them may not even be working there anymore. I could ask...and here she stopped. William hadn't returned home after the argument and no one knew where he was either. She looked up as headlights reached the front window. "Are you expecting someone?"

"Not that I know of."

Susan's heart missed a beat. The door opened. She saw the bald head first and then the perfectly pressed pants and green polo shirt.

"Hi," he began, closing the door behind him and strolling over to his wife.

"What are you doing here!?" she shouted, not taking his hand, but stepping slightly away from him.

"What is *she* doing here?" William demanded.

"*She* happens to be my daughter and we've been discussing all of the possibilities of where Kate might be."

"Oh." He barely looked at her and sat in the straight back chair opposite the couch. Everyone stared at him. So, this is how William would return from wherever he had been for days on end. Placing his manicured hands on his lap, William began brushing at his slacks—for lint that wasn't there, probably.

"So, who else did Kate know at Jenkins Fidelity?" Susan asked.

Her mother jumped. She avoided William's gaze.

"Many. It's a pretty big place."

"Anyone in particular that she befriended?"

William blushed slightly. "Well, there were the gaggle of girls that always ate together, but really, no one that she would go back into hiding with."

"Other than you," Susan added blandly, regretting the words even as she said them.

"I know you don't trust me, but believe me I am as concerned about Kate as you both are. For whatever reason, she has decided to lie about me. And now that she is gone, my mind has been crazy trying to figure out what has happened to her. I drove to all of the places I knew about but no one could tell me anything. Until now. I think I finally have a lead."

"A lead!" Susan shouted. "Well, what is it?"

William continued to stroke his pants. "I've just spoken with Frank Olmstead," he said.

"What?!" Susan's heart thundered. Frank? The jewelry salesman, the same salesman who was a friend of Bob's and spied for him in her behalf?

"Look, the man knows things, always has. When he was following you, Susan, telling Bob about all the places you were going and the people you were seeing, I sometimes doubted what he knew, but no matter what, no matter where you went, no matter what time of day or night you were there, Frank knew about it. I don't know how he knew, only that he knew. And then, today, I realized how many people had once worked for Frank. They are all in prison now—at least most of them."

"Most?" The words squeaked from Susan's lips before she could stop them.

"You remember a David Clariton?"

"Ephraim's friend from South Hampshire?"

"The very same. He's out of prison now."

"What?"

"He was forging documents, like Kate and I, but it was also discovered later that he was selling drugs. His sentence was a bit longer than ours, but just last week, the man was released."

"And Frank, when will he be...?" She began counting the months on her fingers.

"He's due out soon, probably in the next few days."

Susan could hardly believe it. "But...how do either of these men know Kate?"

"Like I said..." The man known as William brushed a hand across his bald head. "David had the same forgery...problem and Frank, well, selling fake jewels has a way of fitting in with the former...ah...sin."

"So you believe David has taken Kate? Why would he want *her*?"

"I wondered that myself. Perhaps he was interested in getting some help; perhaps he had a new plan and wanted Kate to be a part of it. She was pretty slick when it came to forging documents not easily forged." William looked up for the first time and then back down. Susan did not know what to make of it. Was William lying even now?

***

The children were excited.

"Will you play with me when we get home?" Oscar asked, placing the glove on his left hand and tossing the ball on his right. The bat lay beside him like a treasure. And although it had been a few weeks since they'd all managed to make it to the sporting goods store, instead of one day as Henry had promised, the children were both excited; suddenly forgotten was the re-worked plan in favor of the current gifts.

Even Brianne was smiling. She'd just purchased a new dress and some new shoes to go with the dress. The dress was a sparkly green and showed off her eyes.

Susan had never been so happy, albeit worried about her sister's disappearance. How could two things, the addition of two new children and the loss of a sister, affect her so? Well, that was easy enough to answer. She'd waited years for Brianne and Oscar, and Kate? She'd been her sister for more years than she liked to count. Where was she?

No one had been able to find David Clariton, the man who had worked with Ephraim Humphrey—his home had been vacated with no forwarding address and Susan wondered once again if William was merely giving them something to do to take their minds off him.

This idea seemed so logical to her that she decided to talk to Henry about it. And he agreed. The story was almost too far-fetched, even for William, who prided himself in the details of life as did her mother.

William had been allowed to stay home after his return, but Susan wondered how her mother was doing with him, hoped that he was treating her right, or at the very least, with a basic respect that everyone deserved.

A month and a half later, Henry had some news. Her sister had been found.

News

"Henry, you can't mean it!"

The words had shocked her, numbed her, created that aching heat inside her heart that she'd felt a month and a half prior when the word had come that Kate was gone. And now, she was dead?

"Found her in South Hampshire, near the Clariton place."

"But we were just there!"

"Out back..."

"Don't tell me..."

"You will want to know how she died."

Susan didn't want to know how it had happened, not any of it. The baby was gone, too. And it seemed so shallow, all of the thoughts she'd had of her sister only wanting money and nice clothes and a life Susan could never have. And now she was...gone.

"I can't do this!" Susan shouted. "I mean it. My sister is not...gone."

"She was poisoned, Susan."

"Poisoned. How? Where?"

"The same way Bob was poisoned. At least, that's what forensic believes. They're checking into it, but the liquid looks the same. In a clearing, out back of the house we found some sticky goo that had long since dried up but there was some mixture left, on a rock..."

"Shut up! Please, shut up!"

She hadn't meant to explode, but this was her sister, her only sister. And she was dead. Her mother, what would she say—do? Susan didn't want to think about it. She didn't want to think about how her sister must have looked lying dead inside the tall weeds, half buried, the rock only inches from her perfect face. She didn't want to hear that she'd more than likely killed herself because of the turmoil. But that couldn't be right. She'd been at the home of David Clariton after all. Had he proven to be even more deadly since his release from prison? His court appearance and later jail time had obviously occurred after she'd left for Hawaii, though Susan tried to recall the trial she'd attended and how David had moaned about Ephraim Humphrey's problems with drugs and forgery, as well as his issues with women. David, himself, had his own problems, none of them good. Had the man actually taken her sister's life for some reason?

Susan sat on the bed and sobbed. Hours later, she felt numb and slipped into sleep.

***

The funeral was quiet. Her mother sat still, her hand within William's. Neither William nor her mother had spoken to them since the word of Kate's death. Susan sat by Henry. To her right, her children, Brianne and Oscar sat rigidly in the high-backed bench.

It wouldn't be long now.

She could hear sniffling just behind her. Previous to the service she had watched him sit behind her, speak to no one and gradually take something from a bag he'd carried in. There were few in attendance and most of those attending Susan knew, but she didn't know this man sitting directly behind her—or did she?

Near the end of the service, there was a loud cough, made even louder by the moment of silence given to the deceased before the coffin was placed back in the hearse. But before that, long before that, there was a cough in the deep, dark silence. When Susan turned to see who it was she was met with the steely eyes and common smile of Frank Olmstead.

So, he was out. But why come here?

Her mother sobbed suddenly and a thick wad of tissue flew to her nose. William's arm reached around Mother's back and, though Susan couldn't see his face, she felt Henry shudder. What was it about that man she had grown to loath? Was it his mistakes? His prison time? Or was there something else, something deeper that created in Susan such fear?

Henry patted her hand. "It will be alright," he whispered, touching her face briefly and wiping away the tears. "We will find out who did this."

Unlike the death of Bob, the death of her sister had created in Susan more than a desire to find the killer. She wanted to find him and kill him herself. The feelings of hate that burned within her made her uncomfortable to say the least. She couldn't possibly kill the man who had murdered her sister, even if she wanted to. But she would hate him, hate him and loathe him for the rest of her life.

William's arm still rested across the shoulders of her mother. Why was she still with him? Hadn't he caused her enough heartache?

Returning her thoughts to Frank, she watched as the pallbearers were called forward to take the coffin to the hearse. Among them, her husband, William and fellow work associates Susan didn't know. Frank Olmstead was not among them, though she could almost feel his breath behind her as she waited for the service to end and for the trail of cars that would soon be finding their way to the burial plot.

Family that she hadn't seen in years followed the coffin out, but she talked to few of them and tried to adjust her smile at appropriate moments as she thanked one and then another for their attendance.

And then a hand reached out.

She turned.

"So, it's really you," she said.

"I'm sorry about your sister," Frank offered.

He was the same man—almost. He was still red faced and freckled, though his blond hair had a few white streaks and his once frog chin was filling out to make two frog chins. Still, those same bulging eyes blinked at her and it was all Susan could do to breathe evenly. The man had gained some weight since their last meeting at the courthouse, but it was definitely Frank Olmstead.

"I didn't know you knew her," was Susan's reply. Henry reached for her arm. "This is, ah, Henry," she said.

The man reached forth his arm, pumping the hand of Henry. "Glad to meet you," he said. "It's about time Susan got a winner."

Susan was embarrassed. If there had been a rug on the hot, baked cement in front of the church, she would have buried the stupid words quickly underneath it. As it was, the comment floated above her head and it was all Susan could do to try and think of something else.

But it was no use. Suddenly and without warning she was thinking of them all—in that other life she'd lived; Ephraim Humphrey, the man who'd killed her only friend at the time—Ms. Martha Boaz, the owner of the old hotel, Carter Childs and even Mr. Davis, though he was dead now and would no longer be a burden to her.

"Kate and I were merely brief acquaintances, made so when you were off gallivanting and your...I mean Bob needed to know where you were."

Susan must have paled. She could feel the blood leaving her face.

"I'm sorry, we have to go," Henry said, pulling Susan away.

"Just wanted to give you my condolences," the man offered.

"Thank you," Susan forced herself to say.

"And to tell you something in confidence," the man suggested.

Susan turned.

"This is not the time or the place, but I think I have some fine information about Bob and Kate, if you know what I mean. Can we meet sometime?"

"Ah, sure."

Henry's grip tightened on her arm. "I'll be there, too," he said.

"I wouldn't have expected any less," Frank said, leaving them.

***

"Who was that strange man?" Brianne asked. They'd returned home, only to find that rain had fallen and a window had not been shut. As Susan mopped up the wet mess, her children sat on bar stools and the questions came like bullets.

"Why did he talk to you?" Oscar said.

"He looked mean," added Brianne.

"And like a frog."

Susan coughed.

"Did your sister know him?" Oscar asked.

"I guess so. He just wanted to make sure that I was alright."

"Dad looked mad." Oscar had been calling Henry 'Dad' for a few days now and the sound of it felt good to Susan's ears.

"He was just worried about me."

"Are you missing your sister terribly?" asked Brianne, standing beside her now. She could feel an arm around her waist.

"Yes."

"Even though you argued a lot?" asked Oscar.

"We did not—Okay, we argued, but all siblings argue."

"I told you so," said Oscar. "I told you that we're not the only ones."

"What's this really about?" asked Susan. The water now mopped up, she sat down on one of the kitchen chairs.

"I'm scared," said Brianne. "Really scared."

Oscar rolled his eyes and walked to the sink.

"Why are you scared, honey?"

"That man looked mean and he reminded me of somebody."

"Who, honey?"

"Just someone."

"Your father?"

She looked up, tears streaming down her small cheeks. "No, not him. One of the men in the black suits."

Memories of the past hit Susan like waves from the ocean, crashing and heaving themselves across the banks.

She remembered the men who had questioned Brianne and Oscar as they stood outside their ramshackle house long ago—Captain Broadbank's men—and Mr. Davis, now dead. Frank Olmstead, the jewelry salesman, had never spoken with them, had he? Sure, he was a friend of Bob's—he'd watched her and he'd naturally seen the death of Ms. Martha Boaz from the hotel window. She remembered feeling at ease as he'd left the stand that day after his testimony in court. But the man did have a drug problem and he did know Bob.

What had Bob been involved in? Was it bigger than his scheming with William over an already purchased house? Forgery had placed her sister in jail with William. And Bob had somehow escaped it all. But had he in the end?

Dark Memories

"We need to go over some paperwork," Susan said.

"I know. I'll do that today."

"Are you taking the children to school?" It was Monday and school continued, whether she wanted it to or not. Winter was in full force, especially in the morning and continuing throughout the day like a child not willing or wanting to let go.

She was the child and as her newly adopted children headed to the bus for another week of school, she cried. Hoping they hadn't seen her, she bundled herself up once more and headed home, dreaming of the time they'd return and she wouldn't be tumbling inside the house alone.

Just two weeks into school after the adoption, it had hit her, along with her sister's death and the many, many questions she still wasn't able to answer. Perhaps she'd been too eager to hand the business over to Jane Dove. Now, with the empty hours in the morning, she wondered if she should go back—at least part-time.

Henry would laugh and remind her of her promise, she was sure. And by the time summer hit once more, she'd be wrapped up in worry about not being able to spend time with the children. It was better to stay home.

She focused on cleaning and then, feeling as if she should do something to help Henry, listened again to the message left on the telephone. Henry hadn't heard it yet, but the message had only come yesterday:

Susan, this is Frank. I'm serious about meeting. You name the time and place. And bring your husband. Call me.

Susan listened to the message again and it was if she was hearing it for the first time. After the funeral, her husband had demanded that they meet together whenever Frank called. If it was important, Frank would contact her again. When he did, she was to call him. Until then, she was to keep the doors locked and her telephone close by.

But she hadn't told Henry he'd called yesterday in the early morning hours when everyone was still asleep. She hadn't said a word.

She dialed the number.

She could almost see his frog eyes blinking when he said, "Hello."

"This is Susan," she said.

"I'm glad you called. Where will we be meeting?"

"At *Rich's Delicatessen*. You know it?"

There was a slight pause. "Why sure."

Susan's heart beat like a wicked thunderstorm, but she didn't care, or didn't think she cared. By the time her husband was home so would be the children and then they'd probably be waiting until the weekend to meet with Frank. She just couldn't wait that long.

Gathering her coat, Susan trudged to the car. The driveway had been shoveled by her husband before he'd left that morning and it made the pull from the garage that much easier. But it had snowed last night and heaps of the white fluff were layered on the streets in which she traveled until she hit the main road. After that, it was smooth riding, if you considered that she still had to watch for the unseen—black ice.

Rich's wasn't too far off the beaten path but it still took her twenty minutes to arrive and she hoped, no prayed that Frank Olmstead hadn't given up on her too soon. Having parked the car she went inside and looked around. The place was a greasy spoon joint and all Susan could think about was her sister working here. She spied Frank at the back. He was already eating.

She sat across from him on a bamboo chair with a torn cloth seat and looked over at him. "What do you have to tell me?" she asked.

He looked up. "Where's your husband?" His bulgy frog eyes blinked.

There was a distinct smell of grease and other unmentionables that Susan tried to avoid focusing on. In front of her was the man who might just be able to answer some of her questions, about her sister's death and the man her sister was supposed to have fallen in love with.

"I decided not to bring him," she said honestly. The truth was, her husband would have made this visit all the harder. He'd be so worried about her she'd probably forget all of the questions she had.

"Just as well," said Olmstead, picking at his teeth. "Going to order anything?"

"I've already had lunch," she said, removing her right hand from the sticky table and placing it on her lap. "You go ahead."

"Why don't you at least order a drink," he offered, blinking over at her again.

"I'm fine." A waitress walked up in just that moment and planted a glass of water in front of her. "What you'd be ordering?" she asked.

"Nothing right now," Susan said, trying not to make a big deal out of it. "I'm really not that hungry."

"Suit yourself." She turned and left them and Frank looked up from his pizza.

"So, why did you choose this place if you're not even interested in eating?"

"Maybe I prefer diamonds," she said, smiling.

Olmstead chewed. He looked somewhere far beyond her and back. "Your sister worked here, didn't she?" he asked.

"How would you..."

"Now, Susan, I know you pretty well and I know your sister pretty well, too. Until the death of your first dear departed, I had quite the time trying to keep track of both of you."

Susan's heart stopped. It was as if she'd just taken a bite of Frank's horrid looking pizza. "What?" she asked.

"You heard me." Frank wiped his greasy mouth on a nearby napkin.

"You've been following my sister?"

"And you."

"Why?"

"Now, Susan, you know that's the sort of stuff I do." He grinned and Susan could see bits of pepperoni stuck between his teeth. "Your sister, Kate, was a real looker, you know. Better looking than you, though you're nothing to forget to write home about."

"Tell me what you know."

"Your hands are shaking. Are you nervous...Susan?"

"No, I mean, yes. Just tell me what you know about Kate and William."

"Strange pair those two. Not in love, then in love, then not in love again."

"Was the baby William's?"

Olmstead laughed and took a sip of soda. "You know, Susan, you sure do ask a lot of questions. Since I invited you here, wouldn't it just be better to listen to what I have to say?"

Susan doubted it, but she had little choice. "Then, tell me," she said again. This time, she waited until the man had doused a few more gulps and had almost finished his entire pizza. The sitting without speaking was difficult, but the smells inside the room were even worse. How could her sister have dealt with working in such a place?

Finally, Frank looked up from his almost clean plate and stared at her. "Marriage suits you," he said. "I wish your sister had done as she was told."

Susan almost spoke then, but Frank put a greasy forefinger against his lips. "Listen, Susan. What I'm going to tell you now you'll only hear from me once. And if you try to find me after today—if you think that somehow your dear Henry or the police will be able to find me—think again. I am not really even here today—with you. If I know you, Susan, your husband doesn't even know you've come to meet with me. And that message on the machine? I don't think you'll ever let him see it. You wouldn't want to cause him any trouble, now would you, with his heart condition and all..."

Tears welled in Susan's eyes. She tried to blink them away without success.

"Oh, Susan, Susan. Or should I call you Jenny? Well, at any rate, your Kate, your dear sister was murdered. I think you know that. But what you may be wanting is more information than you currently have."

Susan breathed deeply.

"Kate and William met at work. This you know. Kate fell in love with the masterful William, just like he wanted her to. Kate was easier to work with when we had her wrapped around someone's finger. I think she would have married William, too, if she hadn't been foolish enough to find herself interested in someone else. William was angry when he found out she was...expecting. His plan had failed. All he could do now was move forward without her."

"So, William killed Kate."

The frog eyes blinked. "No."

"What do you mean, no?"

"Just what I said."

"So, who killed my sister?"

Frank stood. "Didn't I tell you not to speak? Didn't I tell you to listen?"

"Sorry, Frank. Sit down and continue your story." The man had turned even more strange since she had first known him at the *Hotel Camaro*. Now, his actions were bordering on some sort of mental delirium.

"It's too late for me to sit," he said, turning from her. "Too late."

Susan stood. "Wait!" She grabbed for his arm and attempted to pull him to her. "You MUST tell me."

"Why, Susan? Because again, you have to search for the killer? You have to know who did it just to ease your own conscience? If I told you, right now, in your current state of unbelief, would you believe me? No, dear Susan, you would not."

He blinked at her one last time, shrugged her hand off of his shirt sleeve and turned from her.

"Wait!" she wailed into the restaurant, that was more like some sort of unearthly place, but he was already out the door.

She reached for her coat but not before someone tugged at her own sleeve. "You're not going anywhere!" shrieked the waitress, reaching her. "Someone has to pay the bill."

***

It was time to pick up Brianne and Oscar from the bus stop and as the children descended the stairs, all that Susan could think about was the terrible thing she had done. Henry would never forgive her for this. He would be so angry.

"Did you have a good day?" she asked.

"I guess," said Oscar.

"We had chocolate cake for lunch," said Brianne, taking her hand.

"That's good."

"Can we play in the snow?" Oscar asked as they trudged back to their house around the corner.

"Yea! Let's build a snowman," Brianne offered, tugging at her brother's arm.

"As long as you finish your homework," Susan said. "But your homework has to come first."

"Ah, Mom!" Both children echoed in unison. But Susan knew one thing. Rules, they just had to be followed.

***

Henry fumed. "You did what?"

She sat, staring into nothing. The children were in bed and she and her husband were taking a load off in the living room—*literally* a load off in her case.

"I'm sorry."

"You know, you could have been hurt...or killed. That man can't be trusted. Why did you go without me?"

"I don't know."

Henry looked over at her, his face a scarlet red. "You do so know why. You thought I'd get in the way."

"No..."

"The least you can be is honest," he said, reaching for her hand. "Honestly, Susan. You do the strangest things."

"I just had to know. I had so many questions and I wanted to make sure I could ask them all. As it turned out, it didn't matter that I had questions."

"Why not?"

"I talked too much. Frank got up suddenly and told me he was leaving. He hadn't told me anything!"

"So, you learned nothing."

"Well, not exactly nothing...but... Evidently, Olmstead has been following my sister and I for weeks—more than likely at the request of Bob. Once he was...killed, that man, strangely enough, continued to watch after me and my sister. But why? Olmstead says William didn't kill Kate. But he wouldn't tell me who did. I didn't even get around to asking him about Bob."

"That man is as slick as his hair is greasy," Henry said, touching her cheek. "It's okay, I forgive you."

"I'm so stupid. I've ruined everything."

"When he contacts you again..."

"He won't be contacting me...ever."

She explained how the man had threatened her not to come looking for him—threatened her in no uncertain terms that Henry wasn't to look for him. The police shouldn't be contacted, either.

"Well, that's something we're just going to just have to override," said Henry, taking her into his arms. "We're just going to have to get some help. First, Bob is killed and then your sister. And now Frank comes into the picture with his demands. The police, with all of their unconcern about this case, will just have to step up."

***

Two weeks later, Frank Olmstead was brought into police headquarters and questioned. For all of his 'well-meaning' hiding, the man had not left town after speaking to her and had actually returned to the old place in South Hampshire where Kate had been found dead.

Susan was not allowed in the room when Olmstead was questioned, but Henry was. And he couldn't have been vaguer upon his return.

"Is that it? You questioned him about his involvement with Kate and Bob?"

Henry nodded.

"Well?"

"The case is in full swing now, Susan. Full swing."

"So, what happened?"

"I've been instructed not to tell you."

"So?"

"We can't afford for me to lose my job."

"They would actually fire you?"

"If I don't keep my mouth shut."

Susan squirmed uneasily on the police couch. Okay, so she was reckless at times with her own sleuthing—she sometimes said the wrong thing, did the wrong thing, but her intentions were always good. That had to count for something.

***

The knocking was insistent. It was near noon and the children wouldn't be returning from school for at least three hours yet. Henry was at work, working on the case that she could have nothing to do with. She wouldn't answer, couldn't—Olmstead had been released after questioning—it could be him.

Her heart beat quickly. She stared out the front window. A car was parked just in front of the house. She recognized that car.

Standing, she reached for the side door and opened it.

Her mother glared at her. "So, you're thinking to leave me in the lurch again?" She stomped inside and sat down in one of her kitchen chairs. "What, did you think I wouldn't find out?" She was breathing heavily, as if she'd been running. But that couldn't be it. She was in a sculptured pink blouse, matching boots at her feet. And the coat she was wearing, was it real fur or something manufactured? The whiteness of it almost extinguished the snow still whirling outside.

"What do you mean? What don't you know?"

Her mother's mouth opened then closed. "For the life of me, I can't figure you out, Susan. Your sister was so kind, so generous in everything..." The woman sniffed and retrieved a tissue from her pink purse. "Really, Susan."

If Susan lived to be a million years old—which she naturally quite doubted—this moment would stand engraved on her mind for all eternity. What did her mother mean now? Wasn't it enough that they'd cried together after the funeral? Wasn't it enough that she'd poured out her heart and soul to her mother, though Henry knew nothing of it? What did her mother want from her?

"That man, Mr. Olmstead, Frank, I think. He's out of prison."

"That's no surprise. I talked to you about that."

"He was at the funeral."

"Right."

"And he met you for lunch. You went alone."

"How? I mean..."

"Honestly Susan, I did all I could do to remain quiet. That place disgusts me anyway, but how else was I going to feel your sister close to me? William let me do it. He said it would do me good, so we dressed down, so to speak, and went there for lunch. I talked to quite a few of Kate's friends and they seemed sorry for her passing."

"You what?" Now Susan was confused. Had her mother and William actually stepped within the wall of *Rich's*?

"I saw you with that Mr. Olmstead, how he blinked at you, his big eyes flapping. It almost made me sick. I almost didn't come over here today, but you had to know what I saw."

Susan's heart continued to tick, but at any moment Susan was sure it would stop and she would drop to the ground—dead. "What did you see, Mother?" she asked.

Hope smoothed her polished fingernails against her polyester pants. "It was that David Clariton, friend of Ephraim. You remember him."

Sure, Susan remembered the drug dealer. The forger. But how did her mother know of him?"

"I know you think I'm just an old woman, without a brain inside my head, but I tell you, Susan, David Clariton was peering at you from the kitchen. He must work there and he must have some connection with Frank Olmstead."

Susan couldn't believe it. "How did you know it was David?" She, herself, hadn't seen David Clariton in months and her mother, why, she'd never ever laid eyes on the man.

Her mother blinked at her. "I read the papers during the trial. I saw him outside the courthouse once."

"You were at the trial?"

"Of course I was at the trial. You are my daughter."

"But I didn't know, I..."

"What do you take me for, an uncaring mother? I was there, Susan. I saw all of it."

"But I didn't see you."

Hope smoothed her coat between her fingers, her pink nails glowing. "Of course you didn't. You were so wrapped up in pain that all you could think about was your own skin—and Henry's."

Susan realized she was crying. She wiped the tears from her cheeks and stared at her mother. "I can't believe you were there," she repeated.

Her mother stood and walked to her chair. In the process of Hope's ranting and raving about David Clariton, Susan had also sat down, wondering for the millionth time how little she really knew about her mother.

The Facts

The children wanted to play Monopoly and so the game was strewn across the kitchen table like so many broken pieces of her life. Only, she wasn't thinking of her life now, now that the children were home and her husband was smiling at her from across the table. "Park Place, again," he said, paying his dues and picking up the card.

They'd played the game only a few weeks ago and he'd won with Park Place, Boardwalk and all of the reds. Today it was the blues and yellows.

"Maybe Dad cheats," said Oscar, looking down at his railroad cards. "I want to build something and all I get are these stupid cards."

"I thought you liked the railroads," said Susan, trying to calm his angst.

"I do. I did. But you can't build on railroads."

"I've got greens," said Brianne, snuggling them against her chest.

"You're weird," said Oscar.

"None of that," said Henry. "Let's just play the game."

Brianne placed the cards in front of her and tossed the dice. She reached for her token—a silver top hat—and moved it forward.

Susan smiled when the girl landed on Free Parking. They'd decided on placing all of their money there, whenever the game had them pay their dues, for one lucky lander.

Brianne squealed. Oscar groaned. "I can't believe it. I just can't believe it!" he wailed.

"Well, that's just a part of the game," said Henry. It was a basic comment, one that you'd give a person while playing a game that they weren't winning, but the comment bothered Susan all night. Near 2 a.m. she awoke, gathered up her robe and with slippers on her feet, found a place to relax in the living room. Was sitting back and waiting for word on her sister really just part of the game? Or was it in her sister's best interest for her to do something about it? Her sister had been found dead at the Clariton place, poisoned and all she could do was wait it out?

She lit the fireplace and watched as the red and orange lights flashed before her eyes. What was sleuthing really, but an opportunity to find out the truth. A person didn't need a badge to search out the truth.

The room warmed and Susan stood, nearing the fire. She grabbed a blanket and pillow from the couch and continued to sit, speaking to the fire as if it had all of the answers. If the truth were known, she could go on with her life. Not that she wasn't moving forward now, but her place of business would soon belong to another. She would spend her days cooking and cleaning and waiting for her children to return home from school. And then what?

The ache inside her was growing. Why was it growing? Why wasn't she satisfied to sit back and allow her husband and those at the police station to find the killer? Why?

Was standing back and allowing others to play, really a part of the game called Life?

Susan laughed at her own joke, for surely, there was a game called Life and she knew it then, without really feeling like she'd discovered anything, that she would have to continue in her search for her sister's killer. It was all she could do.

***

Her children tucked tightly in the bus, Susan walked home, the crunch of old snow feeling its way around her boots. She warmed the car, scraped the windows crusted with ice and gathered some of her warm belongings for the drive. She would eat breakfast and possibly lunch in the car and the hat and gloves would come in handy when the occasion presented itself.

South Hampshire, named after the cozy town of Hampshire, England, was a fair trip from New Jersey, still, with the weather such as it was, there would be no room for speeding on already slick roads—though most of the traveling would be by freeway. When

Susan arrived an hour later, she grabbed her lunch, ate the contents within the paper sack and then stared up, quite leisurely at the house.

A small home with yellow vinyl siding greeted her. Though the lawn was snow packed and the windows iced over, she could see that at one time, the house had been quite charming. Though the lilac colored shutters were not really her taste, Brianne would have loved them and would have called the house 'her dollhouse' she was sure of it.

She only had a short time—just about a half an hour or so to walk through the premises and seeing no cars in the driveway, she ventured around the house. Out back was a large yard with an old fence backing the property and plenty of trees. The rock, or at least the rock that had filled Susan's mind for days, met up with her after only a few short minutes walking the property. It sat as if waiting near the back of the Clariton property. She bent down, touching the cold surface and moved a fair amount of snow from around the gray boulder. Grass was underneath it and the snow on top made it patchy in spots. Susan moved as much snow as she dared and when she could see nothing, either on the top or sides of the large stone, she looked away. A voice had caught her attention, just a few feet away from the house.

Looking up, she noticed someone standing in the window, though they were too far away to see clearly. Susan stood from the mound and brushing her gloved hands against her jeans, walked to the house.

In a blink, the person at the window had removed themselves. Where they were now Susan hardly knew, but as she approached the back door it opened.

A woman, probably in her 30s peered out at her from beyond the screen. She looked older than forty, with her long, greasy hair and saggy clothing, but the woman's eyes told Susan otherwise. The woman was in fact fairly young.

Susan stood at the back porch, but the woman remained silent. "I'm sorry for trespassing," she began, looking behind her for only an instant and pointing her finger to the rock. "My sister was killed here."

"So, you're the sister," the woman said, opening the creaky screen. She stood silently, taking in every inch of her and it was all Susan could do to remain planted where she was. A creepy feeling, unlike those she'd occasionally witnessed during a horror movie, entered her back and ran up her spine. Who *was* this woman?

"And you are?"

"Mrs. Clariton. That's all you need to know." She blinked at her—once—then left her standing there, the door still open.

Susan approached the back door. She could see Mrs. Clariton through the back window. She was in the kitchen preparing something. She opened the screen and stepped inside.

The room was as neat and clean as a hospital receiving room. As the woman cooked, her back to her now, Susan looked upon her surroundings. A small table and plenty of plates stacked in cubbies throughout the room met her eyes first. And then, maple cabinets, a black stove and matching fridge. The floor was a cheap Linoleum but it was clean and the place was tidy, even on the far wall where books were displayed.

Mrs. Clariton turned. "I didn't think you'd ever get here," she said.

"What?"

"Sit. I've made some tea."

Susan reached for a wooden chair and sat, watching the woman that seemed creepy one moment and friendly the next.

"It's herbal," she said.

"That's fine," Susan answered, looking down at the warm liquid in a sparkling white cup. "It's cold out."

"I have been dreaming of spring," Mrs. Clariton said. "But my husband won't be coming around here no matter the change."

Susan swallowed, not taking a sip.

"He's really a good man, you need to know that. But sometimes, when money gets tight...well, you know, things get difficult."

Susan looked up at the clock. She had only a few more minutes before needing to return home to pick up the children.

"I'm sorry that your sister was killed—here," she began, sitting down at the table.

"Me, too." Susan took a sip of liquid. The warmth coated her cold throat. The stuff was like peppermint with a dash of lemon.

"I've been wanting to talk to you for some time," Mrs. Clariton added, taking a sip from her own cup.

"Oh?"

"You must be angry at my husband but you shouldn't be. Granted, he's had his problems, but he didn't kill your sister."

"Where is he now?"

The woman stared over at her, her eyes unblinking. "I wish I knew. I can no longer pay the bills and soon, very soon, I'll have to leave this place."

Susan felt bad for the woman. She paused, reflecting for a moment on what she might say—do. Mrs. Clariton was obviously in distress. But she just had to know.

"Do you know a Frank Olmstead?"

Mrs. Clariton coughed. "Oh, yes. He's the one who got my husband in this mess in the first place. That Frank, he can make anyone and I mean *anyone* believe what he tells them. He has swindled us and he's swindled others, too. He plays the act of being a nobody, but you need to know he's not a nobody, he's a somebody and he's the one who killed your sister."

Susan's throat closed off; the warm liquid was no longer working.

"The police?"

"They've been here and they've talked to me, but I haven't said anything about what I'm telling you now."

"How come?"

The woman squirmed. "My husband, he has no idea that I know what I know. Maybe in the beginning, when we were first...in the beginning." She stopped speaking and took another sip. "In the beginning things were different. My husband was different. And Bob..."

"You know my husband, I mean my ex—"

"There was no getting around it. Once Frank was in the picture, so was Bob. I'm sorry about him, too."

"So, who killed Bob?"

"If I knew that, I'd be the best detective on the planet." She tried to smile but the smile was forced. "Susan, you need to know that your ex was a good man until he met Frank. They were buddies in college. My David was a friend to your husband in college. But when things went bad, they really went bad."

"Your sister, when she became part of the mix—that's when things really began to heat up. She was never what she seemed—I'm guessing you knew that. We were friends in college..."

"You were friends with my sister?"

"Of course I don't look anything like I used to—who does? She brushed her fingers through her stringy hair. "But in those days we were quite the pair. We could get any man we wanted. Unfortunately, your sister had it in for an older man."

"William."

"William." She stood now, took her cup to the stove and poured herself another drink. "I couldn't convince Kate that the old guy was wrong for her. I tried everything, even leaving the car in the driveway with little to no gas. She always wanted to see him if you know what I mean and, as far as I know, he never returned the favor."

"He's married to my mother now."

"I know that too. Susan..." And here the woman paused and reached for her from across the table. William can't be trusted."

"Do you think he killed my sister?"

Mrs. Clariton opened her mouth to speak and finally the words came. "Call me Chris—I don't know if William killed your sister, but he had a motive. They were working together, forging...selling drugs..."

Susan looked into Chris' eyes and then up at the clock. It was time to leave. If she didn't, her kids would be standing around wondering where she was. Oscar was old enough to walk home—and had told her so—many times. She figured he was embarrassed. But she had to come to the bus stop for Brianne. She was still so young and Oscar, well, she wasn't quite sure he was responsible enough to take over.

She stood. "I'm sorry, but I have to go. Do you have a phone number I can reach you at?"

Chris frowned. "Not at the moment. In another week the power will be cut off, too."

"What will you do?"

"Go live with family I guess."

Susan reached out a hand. Chris shook it slowly, her fingers hanging leisurely around Susan's. "I will just have to come to you," she said. She reached for her coat that she'd laid across one of the kitchen chairs. "I will be back in a day or two. We can finish our conversation then."

***

Two days later the house was empty. Nothing was left inside, not even the few pieces of furniture Susan had noticed on her previous visit. The place was locked up—tight. She turned from the house and returned to the large rock at the back of the property.

The sun had warmed things up some since her last visit and the grass, yellow and seeking warmth, poked itself from around the boulder. At the back side she saw it, a speck of blood. Her sister's blood. She touched it with her finger and looked on, far beyond the back fence.

What would her sister tell her if she was here? Would she talk about the murder? Would she share with her why she'd come to the Clariton home in the first place? Was it to see Chris, or had she still been involved selling drugs and forging documents for money? If only her sister could answer her questions.

Standing, Susan continued to the back fence. It was then she saw it, a gate leading to the neighbor's yard. Like the blood on the dark rock, the gate had blended quite naturally into the wooden fence and hadn't been distinguishable at a distance. But now, as she lifted the latch, it opened without a squeak to reveal another yard.

Like Chris's home, the house was old and in need of repair. Dressed in white, the old wood practically creaked as she looked at it and entered the back porch. There was no furniture inside here either; the place looked deserted.

Working her way to the side of the house Susan spied another gate. Unlatching it she swung around the house to the right to look on the house properly. What she saw disturbed her even more than finding Chris gone along with her belongings.

On the house, directly to the side of the front door, was a plaque carved from a piece of wood. The plaque read: "Kennedy." Walking to the mailbox, a broken-down thing with a bent pole supporting the box itself, Susan read the words: "Lane Kennedy: 32 Lyndhurst Avenue."

This couldn't be the same African American Lane Kennedy who had used a fake address in Nevada for the gun shop in South Hampshire! Had Kennedy lived here at one time? Walking back to the front door, Susan peered inside. There were no drapes to speak of and the place was as empty as a haunted house.

Had the police checked here? Had they put two and two together? Obviously, if this was the same Lane Kennedy who had been involved in the *Hotel Camaro* case, being a stone's throw away from the Clariton's was an answer made in heaven.

***

"What did Lane Kennedy receive for his crime, do you remember?"

The children were tucked in bed and no one had been the wiser of her sleuthing. Her mother had called her on her return from the Clariton's and she'd lied about doing some shopping. But her mother wanted to see her. *Tomorrow*, she'd said and now that she was speaking with her husband in the living room, she thought again of her mother. She couldn't lie to him, too, could she?

"I think he got six months and had to do some community service," Henry said sitting down and patting the spot next to him. It had been a long day. His red hair wasn't parted evenly and his eyes looked tired.

"I guess the man doesn't really live in Nevada," she said.

"Of course he does, with his wife and four kids." Henry looked at her strangely.

Henry reached for her hand. "Come on, Susan, why all the questions?"

"I went out to the Clariton home today," she confessed, not speaking of her previous visit. She wasn't quite sure if she *could* speak of it.

"You did, what?"

"I know I shouldn't have, but did you know there's a gate out the back leading to the Lane Kennedy property?"

Henry blinked, then his face paled. "You shouldn't have gone there," he said. "The police, they've been staking out that house for months now."

"So you know..."

"Lane Kennedy was living there for a time, but he must have left about the time David Clariton went missing. We were hoping one or both of them would return—especially since not all of them took off together."

"You mean, Chris."

"Who is Chris?"

"The woman married to David."

"When did you meet *her*?"

"Two days ago. Today she was gone and all of her furniture."

Henry stared at her blankly. He stood, pacing the floor. "I should have told you everything," he began, "but I was practically threatened with my life if I did so. I should have known that you'd be curious enough to go searching on your own—especially since I couldn't tell you everything. Maybe it will be alright." He sat, but didn't reach for her.

"Maybe?"

Henry brushed his fingers through his red hair. "With Lane Kennedy released from jail and David Clariton and Frank running around and William still in the house with your mother, I have no idea what's going to happen next."

"Are you worried that William might hurt her?"

"We've worried about that for months now, but with no real proof that he's had anything to do with the two deaths, we have nothing to bring him in on."

Susan reached for her husband's hand and held it firmly. "Well then, you have to have my help. I can get through to people that the police can't, I know that much. When I visited with Chris about Kate and about her husband and Bob, she was quite willing to share with me the details."

"Bob?"

"Evidently, they are all connected."

***

Brianne and Oscar stood, fully dressed and waiting for her answer. "Let's go to the movies!" Brianne sang. Oscar nodded, embarrassed at his sister's remarks, or so it seemed. Just yesterday, she'd ventured to her mother's only to return more stressed out than ever.

When Susan asked her to look around her place for clues that would bring the killer to justice, her mother had wailed: "Susan, You don't think William had anything to do with this!"

"I hope not, Mother, but Bob and William did know each other and there's that bit about Bob swindling William's money. There's also that little piece of forgery tucked away, that connects with our darling Kate."

"I tell you, William was at the club the night Kate went missing. And he was here—with me!"

"I know that, too, Mother. But you've got to understand..."

"...You wouldn't let Kate stay here because you thought that William would hurt her, maybe even kill her..." The color drained from her mother's face.

So, it was finally out.

"...Now everything makes sense. If William is the killer he had a reason for killing both your husband and *my* daughter."

Susan wanted to correct her mother in that moment, but sometimes it was just better to be quiet.

"...I can't believe William is the killer!"

The confession from her mother's lips created a funny sensation in the pit of Susan's stomach.

"What if the man married me to get to Bob? And Kate?"

Susan's own thoughts were whirling. "Now, we don't know that for sure, Mother. We don't know that. The killer could be any of the other men. Olmstead, David Clariton, or even Lane Kennedy."

"You're right, of course." Her mother sat, drink in hand and took a sip.

"Have you been feeling alright?" Susan asked.

Her mother had donned the red pajamas and her hair was left, uncombed, though it was noon.

"I can't sleep and sleeping pills haven't helped," she replied. "William comes and goes—goes mostly. I can't figure him out. One moment he's the doting husband, the man in love with me and the next he's out the door for an entire day, sometimes even two, before he returns."

"He did say he was searching for his own clues."

"Yes, that's what he *says*." Her mother was quiet. Susan waited.

The house was still a tidy representation of her mother, but it felt different, as if God had left it somehow—as if all the discussion about William and Bob and her sister and all of the others, had filtered through the spaces of Hope's very home and had made themselves visitors within the walls.

"I don't know if I can trust him anymore," Hope continued, picking at her red silk pajamas. "I confronted him and he told me that he was innocent of hurting Kate. He told me he was innocent!" A cry of pain filtered through the air and her mother, once regal, once so sure of her abilities and the direction she must take in this life, buried her face in her hands.

Susan blinked. The children were staring at her.

"Why are you crying?" Brianne asked and Susan realized she'd been daydreaming.

"Oh, I don't know. She wiped the tears from her cheeks and stared into the intense faces of her children. Henry hovered above them.

"You've been in dreamland for some time," he said. "So what do you say, the movies?"

Brianne squealed and Oscar took her hand. "Come on Mom," he said. "I'm bored."

Brianne

"I've been watching you, Mom."

"Watching me do what?" Susan asked. The two were loading the dishwasher while Oscar cleared the table.

"When you don't know I am," Brianne answered, taking a plate and placing in the dishwasher.

Susan smiled. "I hope it wasn't when I was somewhere private," she said.

"No, at least I don't think so..."

"She stares at everyone," Oscar piped in, bringing two cups to the counter. "She is always staring at me, too."

"I do not!" the child wailed. "Mom, I only watch you!"

"Watch me do what?" Susan answered. Sometimes the games children played were downright silly, but she would play along. Oscar walked back to the table to retrieve more dishes. Susan could hear the television in the other room. Henry was obviously taking a load off.

"You have been going secret places in the car."

Susan's heart stopped. "How do you know that?" she asked.

"I know you sometimes go to the grocery store, but grandma says you are doing other things I'm supposed to watch. She told me not to tell you."

"When did you see grandma?"

"She came to school last week."

"Why?"

Brianne shrugged. "I got out of class for a couple of minutes and she talked to me about you."

"When was this?" A dish was poised mid-flight.

"Last week. She came by the house, couldn't find you and so came to the school. She thought I'd know."

"It was weird," said Oscar. "I was in class and was called to the principal's office. I didn't even know grandma was on the list."

Susan thought of the names she'd listed in case of emergency. Henry's, obviously and her mother's, just in case Henry couldn't leave work.

"What did she ask?" Susan tried to ask the question as nonchalantly as possible, worried that her daughter, standing as close to her as she was, could hear her frantic heart beating.

"She asked me about that man who talked to us at the funeral. And she asked me if you had friends who lived out of town."

"What did you say?"

Oscar returned to them. "Grandma was all frantic, as if something bad had happened to you. I was relieved when we got off the bus and you were standing there."

"Why didn't you say something—then?"

Brianne sniffed and wiped a stray tear from her eye. "She told us not to, but my stomach kept hurting."

"That's because you're a baby," Oscar said, grabbing for the dish rag and returning to the table to wipe it down. Susan could still hear the television in the distance.

"Your grandma is right. I have been traveling out of town a bit," she began, as Brianne's face turned up to hers, listening. "I will talk to grandma about coming to the school only when it's an emergency."

Oscar slapped the wet rag in the sink. "I was pretty weirded out," he said. "Is grandma alright?"

Susan played her last visit with her mother over and over inside her head. No, her mother wasn't alright, but how could she reveal the same thing to her children? "Grandma is just fine," she said. "She was probably just worried about me. I'll talk to her about it, okay?"

***

The morning she was planning on confronting her mother someone knocked at the door.

Opening it leisurely, she gasped.

Frank pushed himself inside. "Darken all of the windows—now!" he railed. The door slammed and Susan got to work. Fortunately, the children were in school. Not so fortunately, Henry had already left for work. It was 9 a.m.

"Why are you here?" she screamed, trying to button down the hatches as quickly as possible. The kitchen was soon dark.

"The other rooms—now!" Susan ran to the living room and closed the drapes.

"No gaps!" wheezed Mr. Olmstead, blinking his frog eyes.

Susan readjusted the drapes and ran down the hall to Brianne's room. She'd left it a mess once again and as she stumbled to the window, something cracked.

Frank breathed inside the door frame. "What are you grabbing?"

"Nothing, nothing." Susan turned from the window. "I think I broke a toy."

"Don't worry about that now. Get the boy's room!"

Susan brushed past him and shut her son's blue drapes. Tears had begun to well, but she ignored them and raced to the master bedroom.

"Must have some fun in here," the man said, grinning at her as she swept past him. Her hands trembling, she shut the blinds and turned to face him.

"Now that's better. Now we can talk."

Susan plunked herself on her daughter's bed, then thought better of it. "Maybe we should go into the living room," she mumbled.

"My thoughts exactly." Mr. Olmstead's hands pushed something firmly inside his front pockets. He wore a purple shirt, a black tie and jeans. His thick curls framed his fair face. For all intents and purposes, the man hadn't changed since the day he'd barged into her apartment at the *Hotel Camaro*.

"Well, now, how are you doing, Susan?" he asked.

She'd sat across from him on one of the living room chairs. It was a high-backed thing and far too straight for her to be sitting in now. Still, it held her up.

"Better, until you arrived."

Mr. Olmstead blinked. "I've come to sell you some jewelry," he said, reaching inside his right pocket. He pulled out a necklace and it

Susan was not mistaken, it was the same necklace that had one night been slipped into her room at the *Hotel Camaro*.

"Strikes the fear of dread in you, doesn't it?" Frank asked.

Susan nodded, unsure of what he wanted, what he really wanted."

"Does me, too. Imagine, all of the days and—nights, following you and that wicked Ms. Boaz. You were like Mutt and Jeff, no, more like Sonny and Cher." He laughed.

"What do you want?" Her hands wouldn't stop shaking and her lips, suddenly and without warning, began to tremble.

"You were warned, Susan. Warned about speaking to the police. Warned about not speaking to anyone about our visit. And now, your mother knows?"

"How do you know...about...my...mother?"

"I saw her as plain as day and I knew she would let on that she'd seen me there. She's always been a talker."

Always? Susan thought but didn't say.

Frank swung the necklace around his forefinger. It glittered in the otherwise darkened room. "Imagine my surprise when I remembered where I'd put this. And I thought of you. The gift you never really took in as your own."

Susan was startled by the accusation. She—never had really wanted the thing. And now, Frank had it; why did he have it? Wouldn't it still be with the police as part of the investigation?

"I don't want it. You need to leave—now," Susan muttered. She really couldn't demand anything; her voice wasn't working properly.

"I bet you're wondering what I have in my other pocket," he said, grinning over at her. His frog eyes blinked and it was all Susan could do to sit upright in the chair.

Still holding on to the jewels in his right, Mr. Olmstead reached inside his left pocket. Susan's heart thundered inside her chest. She dared not look up at the clock—she'd told her mother 9:15; it was now 9:30. In only moments...

"Worried about your mother?" Frank asked.

"No, I..."

"Tell the truth, Susan. You're always one for lying."

Susan breathed in. If she didn't remember to breathe she was going to pass out and then what would happen to her?

"I was about to visit my mother."

"That's better. How do you think I kept track of you for days on end? How do you think you were never far from my gaze—far from my lips?"

Susan trembled. She could not think. What did Mr. Olmstead want?

Frank opened his left hand. In it, was a small piece of paper about the size that Kate had tried to throw into the trash can—the note about William. Laying the necklace down on the couch, Mr. Olmstead opened the crumpled note and began to read:

Dear family,
You will Think me weak but I don't care. life is meaningless. I Haven't anyone to love, not really. I sit for days on end hoping she'll Come back to me, but she won't. I know That now. I hope she is Happy. I hope I will be where I'm going.
Please Understand. I love my family. Even Though you are really not my family anymore. Thank you for taking me In, but I have to leave you now.
bob

Where did you get—that?" Susan breathed. She felt a bit light-headed and held tightly to the chair's arms.

"Where you keep it."

Susan turned to the book shelf where she'd stored the note in a plastic sheet protector. It had been inside a binder and she hadn't looked at the piece of paper in weeks.

"I thought I'd better get this before the police asked about it again," Frank said. "You know, this note could cause terrible trouble."

Susan wanted to speak but her mouth had closed off.

"What do you think this letter really means?" asked Frank. Susan looked up briefly at the clock. It was 9:45 and her mother hadn't called.

"I... don't...know."

"But I know, Susan. If you tell the cops the truth about this letter, I promise not to hold this jewelry over you." He motioned to the necklace still laying on the couch.

"I don't...know...the truth."

"Sure you do, Susan. You've expressed it many times before. You knew, for example, that the note was a not a suicide note when you saw it; when your mother handed it to you, didn't you?"

"How did you?..."

Frank sat the note down to his left and lifted the necklace. "Some things are just not what they first seem to be. Get my drift?"

Susan watched again as the necklace glittered between Frank's fingers.

"This, dear Susan, is of course not the necklace I gave you. But doesn't it look strikingly similar?"

Susan nodded.

"And don't you think the note—small as it is—and written by a man equally small in thought—might mean something entirely different than what the police think it is?"

Susan reasoned that anything was possible, especially since she knew her ex-husband hadn't committed suicide. To his last breath, he would not give up, even if she never came back to him. She knew that.

"So?"

The man was waiting. *Was this some sort of game? Why put her through all of this when he could just tell her?*

"I can see that you're anxious for an answer," Frank said, laying the necklace down once more and reaching for the piece of paper. Spreading it out with his fingers, he appeared to write on top of the words, closing his eyes—Susan guessed, for effect.

"Tell me!" she finally blurted.

Frank opened his eyes. "You are one crazy gal!" he said. "So, here it is."

"The letter was to tell you all so long and goodbye. It was an 'how should I put it', *I'm tired of waiting for you, Susan, and I'm especially tired of living with your parents, so I think I will go now.*"

Susan stood. "That's right! That makes perfect sense!"

Frank stood, towering over her. "I think you'd better sit down," he said.

Through the sudden excitement and new discovery, it was obvious that Susan had forgotten herself, had forgotten for a brief second who was in the room with her. And for the first time she realized that this man didn't have a gun that she knew of. He hadn't drawn a knife. Nothing but that stupid necklace and letter. What was she so afraid of?

"Why are you here?" she asked again, looking up at the clock. It was 10:15.

"Now that you know the truth, you will stop this search for me. You will lay off, okay?"

It was stupid, somehow, this request; like a child asking for some candy if he cleaned his room. But although Frank didn't have a gun or a knife that she knew of, there was still something terribly dangerous seething under his skin—and she didn't want to find out what that something was.

"Ok, you've got a deal."

"Not even to your husband. Or your mother. As far as they are concerned, you came upon this little bit of information entirely on your own."

Somehow, this idea seemed even more far-fetched than knowing she received the truth from the frog-eyed Frank. But as Frank handed the wrinkled note back to her and walked quietly out the door—with the necklace—there was nothing she could possibly do but believe him.

***

"You broke my toy!" shrieked an inconsolable Brianne. "It was my favorite!"

Susan thought of the china doll her mother had purchased for Brianne at one of those old-time boutiques and tried to be sympathetic to her daughter's tears. The doll, though expensive, had lived on the floor or under the bed more than it had been displayed on the shelf since Brianne had received it. And now the head was broken.

After Frank had left her, she'd had a difficult time opening the blinds and drapes throughout the house. What if he was still looking? What else might Frank know the he wasn't telling her?

Brianne touched the doll's dress and tried to fit the broken head back on the body. "Maybe Dad can fix it," she said.

But Susan wasn't sure. There were at least three breaks and many more slivers of pieces ground into the carpet than they'd been able to find.

"Sorry," she said at last. "I didn't know she was there."

Brianne looked around her room. "Why are the blinds shut?" she asked.

"I just wanted to keep the house—warmer," she lied.

Just that morning, as Frank had wandered into her home, the flurries had begun. After he'd left she'd briefly checked the kitchen window, only to discover the snow had finally stopped after his departure.

Not daring to leave the house—yet—she'd called her mother's cell phone only to have a message repeat into her ear. She'd picked up the children from the school bus a little uneasily and now was waiting for the return of her husband.

In the meantime, Oscar had wanted to play outside. Against her wishes, he was out in back making a snow fort. And now, Brianne was getting on her boots.

"I'd rather you not go out," she said. "It's pretty cold."

"I want to help Oscar."

Peering out her daughter's window, she watched again as her son began to create another wall for the fort. A slight tug on her arm made her turn. "Don't worry, Mom. I know you didn't mean to break the doll. I'll just ask grandma for another one."

Revelation

"Had a visitor today, I see," Henry said, setting his briefcase down and wrapping her in a tight hug. "Who was it?"

"A visitor?"

"Someone with big feet."

"Mom," she said.

"She must have been wearing boots."

"Well, there is snow out."

He shrugged. "What's for dinner?" he asked.

"Tacos."

"Need any help?"

The hamburger was already cooking on the stove, but she hadn't chopped the tomatoes yet, or for that matter, sliced the avocado's. "Would you really like to help?" she asked. The children were still building out back and at last look the walls were looking pretty steady, something she wished that she felt inside.

"Sure." Henry got out the cutting board and reached for the tomatoes. "How was your day?" he asked.

Her heart pounded. "Fine, I guess," she lied.

"Still having problems being alone all day inside the house?"

"I guess."

"Where should I put these once they're chopped?" he asked.

She reached for a bowl and handed it to him. "I really appreciate the help," she said. "You've spent so much time at the computer."

"Sorry about that." The chopping sound and Henry's soothing voice made her forget Frank for a moment. Weird and scary Frank. How could she tell Henry?

"Where's the avocado's?"

"Here." She reached for them by the side of the refrigerator. "They're a bit squishy, but I can never get the avocado's just right. Either they're too hard and so I set them out, or they're too squishy to begin with and I probably shouldn't have bought them."

"Hard heads are like that too," Henry said. "It takes some real reasoning to soften them up."

Susan laughed, the first laugh she'd had all day. "Where did that come from?"

"Probably all the work I've been doing. I guess I'm just not cut out for an office job." He paused and sliced open the avocado. "You know, hard-boiled eggs can be good, but if you always eat them that way, life can get pretty boring."

"Now, you're really weirding me out," she said. The hamburger was cooked. She took it off the burner and began to shred the cheese. "What's all this talk about avocado's and hard-boiled eggs anyway?"

"Just a thought I've been having recently, about people, about getting them to speak out about what they know, which they don't do, of course."

"Of course." Susan breathed in slowly, taking in the texture of the lettuce leaves as she broke and tore them into small pieces. "I wish I knew something, anything," Henry offered.

"You mean about my sister and Bob?"

"The police want to see that note again, you know the one that Bob wrote."

"It's still in the binder—" she began and then stopped. Yes, it was in the binder, but the thing was a crumbled mess. How would she explain that?

"I'll go and get it out after dinner. That Frank Olmstead, he never called you, right?"

Susan swallowed—hard. "Let's get the food on the table. Everything's ready."

"I'll go get the kids," her husband answered, leaving her for a moment and then turning around. "You didn't answer me. Frank never called, did he?"

She shook her head.

***

Three days later, the weekend in full swing, she watched Henry in the living room reading the newspaper. Nobody read the newspaper anymore, unless they read it online, but Henry was old-school, or old something. He preferred the paper.

The air outside was a cool and wintery as that day Frank had come for his surprise visit and, as yet, Susan hadn't said a word. But what would she say that wouldn't make her dear Henry blush in a heated frenzy? She still worried about his heart condition, though he took care of his health better than he ever had.

She'd already spilled the beans about meeting Chris. And her husband had had a million questions to ask her after that. She'd even had to go to the police station—just once, mind you—to tell them what she'd discovered. Boy, had she been reprimanded. She was not to go sleuthing on her own, she was to stay home, stay put and she'd done that. Now what?

Could she tell her husband that her mother knew that Frank was still hanging around and, in fact, had pushed himself into their very home?

Henry was on a journey of his very own and although they'd spoken some about the case, she knew he was still holding back. Well, she could hold back, too.

She wanted to share with Henry everything, but how could she and not get him into trouble? Her mother, once sane though eccentric, was acting out in ways that not only surprised but worried her.

Confronting her mother about what had happened had only sent her into a turmoil. "They what?" she'd shrieked. "Really, Susan, why would I go to your children's school, ask them to leave class and then ask about your whereabouts?"

"Well, did you?"

Her mother had paled at that moment. "I remember thinking that I wanted to go over to the school," she began, "but I couldn't reconcile doing so. In the end I gave up on the idea."

"You couldn't have given up. Brianne and Oscar said you were there. They were both taken from their classes and you stood there in the office asking them questions. They were told they were to say nothing to me. And now, you're denying it, too?"

"I don't know, I just don't remember," Hope had faltered, sitting down.

And now, Henry was sitting in the living room reading the paper and all she could think about was how awful she was lying to him.

"Honey?" she began.

He looked up. "What?"

"Can you put the paper down for a minute. I have something to tell you."

She began with the story of her mother at the school and ended with the visit from Frank.

"When did this happen?" He looked surprised. Even flabbergasted.

"Last week. I'm sorry I didn't tell you."

"Something's got to change." Henry stood, whisked a rigid hand through his red hair and paced the room. "I don't get it, Susan. We were supposed to be working together."

"Together? You mean even after the police questioned me like I was the killer?"

"They didn't question you like you were the killer. I was in the same room, remember?"

She remembered. But she also remembered how angry they'd been at her and the veiled threats she'd received as Henry had looked on.

"Why didn't you stop them from asking?" She wasn't sure, but Susan was almost positive Henry had stopped breathing in that moment. A sharp intake of breath had come into her ears and his red face had paled to an even white. "I'm sorry," he said. "I should have known you'd take the questioning that way. So sorry."

Interestingly and maybe even because of her mother's plight and the intrusion of Frank Olmstead, she'd almost forgotten about the interrogation—such as it was. Still, she couldn't hide anything that might help Henry discover the killer if she could help it, so why had she?

"I'm sorry, too. I'm just so afraid about you losing your job."

"It's a bit too late for that I think. My last day was today."

"What?"

"I didn't want to ruin dinner. I didn't want the children to be upset. I didn't want you to get upset. I've been sitting here with this paper for the last hour not even reading a word."

He laid it down and looked deeply into her eyes. She remembered this look, too. The look he gave her that said it all, all the pain, all the sorrow that they'd already shared in their lives together—as well as all of the love he still held for her, close to his heart.

Proving Time

All last evening they'd discussed the job loss, what this would mean for their family and what they'd be doing next. Since they hadn't given Jane Dove *Honesty House* yet and the place was still bringing them in a fair income, Henry suggested he take over for a while there and give Jane a break.

Months earlier, Jane would have loved such an offer, but Susan wondered if she would feel the same now. Jane ran the books, she was in charge of all the staff, she dealt with all of the issues that came about whether inside or outside the establishment. She dealt with all of the donations that were finally coming in at a steady pace. Would she relinquish this power after all of the months she'd had it?

Susan was about to find out.

The place was orderly, perhaps even more orderly than when she had first left it. Jane was at the welcome desk and she was talking to a couple of children when she arrived.

Her boots had been stomped at the main entrance, still she knew she was leaving muddy, wet prints.

"Sorry," she began and watched as Jane looked up and smiled. She looked tired and bent down one last time to talk with the children. "Do you have a minute?"

Her friend smiled. "Haven't seen you in awhile. Is everything okay?"

Susan gave her a weak smile and Jane led her into the main room. There were more children today, probably because of the weather and Susan wondered briefly how many more months of the cold she'd have to deal with. If last year was any guide, at least a couple more. They would be well into February before she'd begin to see any change.

They sat at a nearby table. "How have you been?" Jane asked.

"Oh, good," Susan answered, thinking of her husband and her dear children, the only positives in her entire life. "You?"

"I don't know. The children are great, of course and everything is moving forward as good as one might expect...but..." The look in Jane's eyes made Susan lean in closer.

"You're not having any problems?" she asked.

"Oh, no, no. But I've met someone."

"You have?"

Jane smiled. "Just two months now and we're planning our future together."

Susan was impressed and more than a little worried. "Are you sure you've known him long enough?" she asked.

Jane laughed. "About as long as you knew Henry before you married him."

Susan smiled. "What's he like?" she asked.

"Oh, he's a gentleman alright and he has a sense of humor that just won't quit. He can be silly, too. I think I love that best about him."

The man sounded like a good choice, seeing as how Jane was more of the serious type.

"And well, once we're married, I'm afraid he'll be taking me away from here."

Susan supposed this day would come, or did she? Had she always planned on Jane getting her out of tough scrapes, filling in where needed and practically taking over her life when things became too difficult?

"So, you've decided not to buy the place."

"I'm sorry, Susan. I've been thinking about how to tell you for days and when you showed up, I knew that it was now or never." She smiled again, reaching for Susan's hand. "You don't hate me, do you?"

"Of course not. Actually, Henry has lost his job..."

"Oh, Susan, I'm so sorry!"

"When is the wedding date?"

"February 14."

"Wonderful. I hope I'm invited."

"You're both invited. And your children, of course. I was hoping to have the ceremony here."

"What a great idea!"

"Do you really think so?" Jane released Susan's hand and stood. We can stand over there by the fireplace and set up the chairs here (she pointed in the immediate vicinity). The stairs to the second floor could be decorated with flowers, don't you think. Imagine me walking down the stairs and coming to stand next to my beloved."

"Who is?"

"Oh!" A slight hand fell to Jane's lips. "His name is Conrad."

***

The drive to the Clariton's home was first on the agenda. Her husband had been pleased that *Honesty House* could still be theirs and for all intents and purposes, it always had been. Running *Honesty House* might be a new adventure for Henry, but she knew all of the ins and outs of the business and could help him along until the time came for him to take it on full-fledged.

"So, you said that Chris, David's wife, was concerned that her husband had had nothing to do with either murder. That he was just at the wrong place at the wrong time."

"You could say that." The ice was thick on the roads today as Susan shared with her husband once again the details of her visit with Chris.

"She must have been very afraid," Henry said now. The car veered slightly to the right as they turned onto the on ramp and began their journey. The windows, once a foggy glow, had relented their power to the car's heater. Things were getting toasty, despite the weather outdoors.

"What do you hope to find at the Clariton's?" she asked.

"The day before I was—let go, I heard some talk near the restrooms. It seems that Lane Kennedy and this David Clariton have been snooping around both places recently—looking for what, I do not know."

"Maybe Chris took off—you know. Maybe she didn't wait for her husband to return for her. She seemed pretty upset that she wouldn't be able to spend much more time at the house."

"So, you think she left before either of them found her? Maybe that's why they keep coming back."

"I wonder. I mean, Chris was pretty upfront with me, she really wanted to clear the air that it wasn't her husband that had had anything to do with Bob or my sister."

"Maybe she was so insistent because she wanted you to believe he was innocent."

"Maybe. You know, we talked about meeting again and that I'd have to find her because she wouldn't be able to leave a telephone number—hers was being disconnected. But if you were Chris and you had to deliver a message without a phone call, how would you do it?

"Exactly!"

"So that's why we're going to the Clariton's?"

"That, and I need to do some more snooping at the home of Lane Kennedy."

Though they'd left early, right after Brianne and Oscar had stepped on the bus, the icy roads and the snow that had occasionally made its appearance on the windshield had slowed their journey some. Still, driving up the snow encrusted driveway was no picnic either. As Henry pulled up, he turned to Susan. "I hope we don't get stuck," he said.

Susan got out of the car. The snow was deep and reached the bottom of their car. She peeked back inside. "I think you may be right. Try backing out. I'll clear the way."

"With what?"

She looked around but saw nothing.

"Tell you what. Let's dig ourselves out when we leave. Who's to say how much more snow we'll get before the day's done. Fair enough?"

Susan nodded and shut the car door, looking around her. "What if there are some undercover cops watching us?" she asked.

"Checked that on the way in," Henry offered, brushing his red hair from his eyes. "All the cars were empty."

Susan sighed with relief. "Do you think they'll be back, to check on things I mean?"

"Maybe, but the roads are pretty thick with snow and ice. I can't help but think they'll wait things out until things melt some."

"Are you sure?" She looked up at the house now. It was covered in snow and she could barely see into the windows the snow had traveled so high. "I'm worried. Maybe we shouldn't be here, either."

"You're a worry wart." He walked over to her side of the car and took her gloved hand. They were both decked out in the best winter finery possible and it was all Susan could do to follow her husband to the front door.

"Let's go around back," Henry said when, not surprisingly, the door was found locked. Walking to the back he tried a second door. "We've got to get inside," he said.

"I know. But we can't break in, can we?" she asked.

"Shhh, I think I heard someone inside," Henry said.

"Wha-" she began, but a gloved hand was drawn quickly over her mouth. "Don't you hear it?" he whispered.

Susan listened but could hear nothing.

"I think you're going crazy," she said, though she kept listening.

"It's stopped."

"Now what?"

Henry jumped. "Did you see that?"

"What?" Suddenly Susan's feet were cold though she was wearing boots—thick and hearty boots that traveled clear to her knees.

"That! The blinds!"

She saw it then, like a flicker, a blink and then it was gone."

"Someone's in there," Henry said.

"What do we do?"

"I'm not sure, the gun..."

"...is in the glove compartment," she finished, wishing at just that moment that one of them had thought to retrieve it. It was stupid, really. She was stupid and Henry, her dear Henry had been at his desk job far too long.

"Maybe we won't need it." He looked at her wearily and Susan swallowed—hard. Are there any windows open?"

"I'll check. Wait here."

Susan shuddered. Henry checked all of the lower windows. When he walked around the corner to check on the windows in front, it was all Susan could do but stare at the window where the blind had moved. She hoped it remained still—at least until Henry's return.

The wait was like hours and when she heard his boots stepping through the crusty snow once more, Susan breathed a sigh of relief.

"All of the windows are clamped shut. I stopped by the car and got this—he pointed to his pocket. Now, we'll be safe."

Susan watched the window. "Look!" she sang. "It... moved."

Without warning Henry hammered on the door. "We know you're in there!" he yelled.

"Come out, with your hands up!" Susan hollered.

"You can't do that," Henry whispered.

"I know. But maybe it will scare whoever it is out of the house."

"That's the stupidest thing..."

The door clicked. Susan looked down at the knob. It was moving. Clutching her husband's coat, she watched as the door creaked open to reveal the face of Mrs. Clariton.

"I... thought it was you," she began, opening the door and then peering around them before ushering them both inside. "Sit, in the corner—there—" she demanded.

The room was bare of anything that Susan could see. And sitting in the corner of the kitchen this time around was a far cry different than the hospitality she'd received the first time. Chris looked terrible. Was it her imagination? Was she wearing the same outfit she'd seen her in just days ago? Her hair looked cleaner, surely but...

Henry sat next to her and watched Chris wide-eyed as she spoke. "I'm so glad you've come back. I didn't know how to find you, not without your kids seeing me or that mother of yours." Chris was crouching down in front of them, her breath as rancid as a dead rat.

"I didn't know what to do. I left here and hid for a few days, but I just couldn't go home to my parent's place, I couldn't."

Chris sounded like a small child.

"I came back here just the other night." She pulled the house key from the bodice of her dirty blouse. "There have been cops watching this place. But I needed to go somewhere where no one would find me."

"Why here?" *This is the first place they'd look,* Susan thought but didn't say.

But oh, was it cold inside the house. There was obviously no heat and Chris had no coat. Susan unbuttoned her own coat and handed it to the woman. A dirty hand reached out. "Thank you," she said, taking it and putting her arms through the sleeves. "You have no idea what I've been through waiting for you, Susan." Her voice shook.

"Waiting for me? I -"

"Shhh, you don't want him to hear you." She looked around and beyond the kitchen windows.

"Who?"

"Frank."

"Frank Olmstead?" Henry whispered, possibly a bit louder than he should have.

Chris huddled within herself, the coat wrapped around her like a baby's blanket.

Susan's arms were cold. Henry handed her his coat, which she put on and together she and her husband looked at the woman they'd found hiding in the old house.

"I have nothing to offer you," she began, "except some information."

"What information?" Henry asked.

"You must be Henry," Chris said.

"Yes, sorry." He reached out his hand. Chris didn't take it.

"My husband is dead. I found him...outside. Near that old shack behind us. The police, they were walking around. I had—" She stopped, gulping. "I had to leave him. What I can't believe is that they haven't seen you yet. As I said, I've had to travel in the dead of night and I haven't brought along a car."

"For whatever reason, the police aren't staking out either house today," Henry said, though Susan could feel him squirm at the words. She wondered if he'd missed something, if, even now, the police were making their way to the door.

"Did you see who killed him?" Henry asked.

"No—I found him. Alone. In back by the gate. He'd been shot. After I found him dead, I left here. When I returned, his body was gone."

"How long have you been away?"

Chris looked at her. "The day after your wife left, David came home. He wasn't very happy with me. He had this huge van and we loaded what we could into it. On our way out, he pushed me to the snow. 'You're not coming,' he said. 'Find a place to sleep.'"

Susan couldn't believe it. She looked at the sorrowful woman, wondering what she would do in the long-term, without a place to stay.

"Frank, he was here, too. He didn't say much, but his eyes were constantly blinking at me as if he wanted to say something. He and David left me here. I went in the direction of my mother's place after that but I couldn't do it—without a coat, without money. I finally decided to come back here and cut my losses. If they found me, so be it. If they didn't I might still find you."

"I'm glad you did. And I bet you're hungry," Susan said.

Chris blinked. "Very," she answered.

Henry stood and walked, hunched over, to the back door. "I'd like to take a quick look at the Kennedy place before we go, if that's okay," he said. "And then we'll get you something to eat."

"I can't go in there," Chris answered before Susan could speak, "but you go. I will be here when you're finished." She smiled slightly, pulling her dirty fingers through her knotted hair.

Henry reached for Susan's hand. "Let's go, then," he said.

"Maybe I should stay here with Chris," she answered.

"No!" the woman shouted and then recovering from whatever had made her upset, she reached forth to Susan and patted her lightly on the arm. "I will be fine. I am much warmer since I got your coat."

The feeling was strange, though the comment seemed natural enough. "I guess I can come with you if you think you'll be alright," Susan said, looking into Chris' eyes and then into the eyes of her husband.

"Good, then, let's go. We'll be back for you in a minute."

Even as her Henry said the words, there was something about the situation, something about Chris that just wasn't adding up.

The door creaked some as Henry opened it and together they walked through the snow to the Kennedy's. Susan looked back only once to see the blinds move.

At the back door, Susan stopped. "I'm afraid," she said.

"Hand me the gun. It's in my coat pocket," Henry said.

But that only made matters worse for Susan. She reached for the cold steel within her husband's pocket and handed the thing to Henry. "Would you rather wait in the car?"

Susan shook her head. "I'd rather be with you."

He waved her on. As in the Clariton house, looking through the windows proved fruitless. But surprisingly, the front door wasn't locked and as she and her companion walked in, Henry reached for his gun.

The place was empty. Except for a few stray cans and crumpled papers huddled in the corners, the place had been swept clean.

Henry brushed her behind him. "Wait!" he said between clenched teeth. "We're not alone."

"Who's there?" he called into the house—the house that only moments before had held nothing but garbage. She couldn't hear a thing and as Susan stood behind her husband, the gun before him like a talisman, there was a clunk.

"I've got a gun!" Henry hollered.

The noise was palatable now. It sounded like a chair had fallen against the wooden floor.

Footsteps entered the hall. "I have a gun!" Henry repeated, pushing Susan behind him again. "Get out of the house—quick!" he whispered. "Now!"

Susan's mind reeled. She stepped back and was almost to the front door when a large, polished boot stepped into the main room where her husband held the gun. And in the next split second she saw the man's nicely creased slacks and all that went with it, enter the room.

"William!"

William smiled beyond the gun. "You?" Henry asked, his arm relaxing.

"You can see I have no weapon of my own."

"What are you doing here?" Susan asked, still standing behind her husband.

"Same as you, I suppose."

"And what is that?" Henry asked, the gun at his side. He turned back toward her. "You'd better get Chris," he offered. "I can take care of William."

"Chris?" William muttered, easing his way around Henry.

Susan blinked. *Didn't the man know Clariton's wife was only a few feet away?*

"You know, Clariton's wife," Henry answered.

"I wondered who was over there," William said, reaching the window. "But I didn't exactly want to check it out, the way things are around here."

Susan watched William's eyes, the way he looked at them, but not really at them. *What was he really doing at the Kennedy house?*

"If you'll excuse me, I think it's about time I return to your mother."

Henry raised the gun. "Oh, no you don't. Not until you answer some questions."

The man walked sideways to the door. "I can't do that," he said, reaching for the door knob. "You won't shoot me anyway, Henry, cop or no—mostly not." He grinned. "I heard about your little set-back. So what are you going to do now, now that you can't be a cop?"

"That's none of your business." The gun held, but she knew as well as William, her husband wouldn't pull the trigger.

William turned the knob. "Now, I don't want you to get frightened," he began, "but that woman across the way is dangerous. I'm a pussy cat in comparison."

With claws, Susan thought but didn't say.

The door opened to reveal the heavy snow and the man known as William stepped out. "I'll be seeing you," he said. "Oh, yes, I'm sure of that."

Through the open door, Susan watched William leave—they both did. He walked up the street and then turned. Henry grabbed for her hand. "Let's follow him!" he yelled, pulling her to the door. He handed her the gun. Warmed from the hands of her husband, she placed it back inside his coat pocket.

***

When they couldn't find William, she and Henry returned to the Clariton place. But the house was as quiet as death.

"Doesn't surprise me," Henry breathed heavily and with a sudden worry, Susan realized how much they had run. "Sit down." But there was nowhere to sit and no Chris. She'd vanished as well.

Henry was pale. She took off his coat. "Here, you need this more than I do," she said, holding it out for him.

But Henry was too winded. "You'd better get me to the car," he said, reaching for her hand. It was pasty and cold and Susan took a deep breath as she put her husband's coat back on her chilled arms and assisted him to the car. Helping him inside, she raced to the driver's side and turned on the ignition.

Only then did she look at the clock.

Time Changes Everything

"The kids!" Susan wailed. It was past 4:00, way past the time she should have picked them up from the bus stop. She put the car in reverse and pushed on the gas. The wheels spun.

She turned to Henry. His body was slumped in the passenger seat.

"Henry!" she screamed. "Henry!"

Susan opened the car door and tried to move the built-up snow from the back tires with her foot, but her efforts were fruitless. She ran back into the car and tried to back out. The tires spun and she could smell burning rubber.

Shutting the driver's side, she raced to the house next door. It was an old brick thing, but the walks were shoveled and there was a car in the driveway. She knocked.

Moments later that seemed like hours, a child answered the door. He was small and had dark hair and small blinking eyes.

"I need a shovel!" she screeched at him.

The boy started to cry.

"It's okay, I just need a shovel!" Susan hollered.

The boy ran from the door. With the door still open, Susan peeked inside. "Can anyone hear me?" she screeched, not caring how she looked, or indeed, how she sounded. *It was Henry, her Henry!*

"Yes?" a man's voice hollered. He wore an old T-shirt and ragged Levis.

"I...I'm stuck and my husband has a heart condition. He's in the car and I don't know what to do!"

The man peered out the door. "You mean at that vacant house? What you doing over there?"

"Nothing, I mean, we're...can you help?"

The man patted his thick stomach. "Why don't you call the police? Your husband probably needs an ambulance."

"Right, right. With the sudden thought that the man must think her crazy in the head for not thinking about that in the first place, she raced back to her car, reached for her cell phone and began to dial the number."

That's when she saw him.

"William!"

"Well, well. Looks like you're in need of some help."

The last digit not yet pushed, he reached for her cell phone and promptly pushed her to the side. "I don't know what it is about women folk, but they're always messing things up."

"Hey!"

The sound of a man's voice reached her ears. Just as she looked up to see the neighbor, she felt the cold-steel of the gun within her husband's coat pocket.

"Stop! Now!" she screamed, holding the gun before her.

William blinked and held up his hands. The cell phone dropped in the snow.

"Dig me out, now, or I will shoot you!"

William stood stiff before her. He didn't move.

Susan's head bobbed as she looked around. They were alone— except for the big man who'd found his way behind William.

"I need help! Henry!"

As the gun shook before her, she watched in amazement as arms the size of tree trunks wrapped themselves around William's middle and he was dragged to the ground.

***

"Henry, it will be alright," she sobbed, though he could not hear her. She had been asked, no commanded, to sit up front with the driver. The paramedics would work on her husband out back.

She breathed slowly, or tried to, as she recalled what had just transpired. The minutes that seemed like hours until the police had arrived and William was handcuffed and led to the vehicle. Moments that seemed like hours, when the ambulance's shrill noise reached her ears and she could see the whirling red lights, her Henry, still collapsed, though alive in the front seat of their car.

"We'll get there as fast as we can, ma'am," the driver had said, though the struggle through the deep snow was fierce. *When would they get there—when?*

Susan thought of the angry face of William, how he'd scowled at her and threatened her with his eyes. She considered the man who had saved her and how he had helped drag William to the police car. She considered the gun now in police custody.

But mostly she thought of Henry.

***

Henry lay still in the bed. He was alive but not conscious. He'd suffered a heart attack. Susan had been informed that Henry's heart condition was related to an enlarged heart. He'd already been through multiple tests to determine the size, muscle thickness and pumping function of his heart, now the doctors were saying another CT Scan and MRI was in order and possibly cardiac catheterization. He was currently taking water pills and beta-blockers and though Henry had kept his alcohol to a minimum, he was still drinking—something Susan wished he hadn't been doing—though she was drinking, too.

The room smelled of antiseptic and worse. Henry was hooked up to more wires and boxes than she could count—including a heart monitor and an oxygen mask.

There were no more thoughts of finding out who'd murdered her sister or Bob. Her children were with Jane. Her mother was probably furious, but there was no way on God's green earth she would have sent them to her mother's. Still, it had been a furious feat, her children waiting for her at the bus stop in the freezing cold and then, not seeing her, traveling home without her and unlocking the front door using the key hidden within the fake rock near the entrance.

She had called them on her cell phone the moment her thoughts had cleared. After Henry had been wheeled into the emergency room, after all of the terror—the wondering if he would die was mostly over—the children had come to her mind. *The children!*

"Oscar, is that you?" she'd breathed into the phone.

For a moment there was silence and then, "Mom! Where are you? We waited for a long time but Brianne got cold! Where are you?"

She remembered his frantic voice and her darling Brianne crying in the distance.

"Are you alright?"

"We're fine. Where are you? Mom, Brianne's scared."

"I'm at the hospital. Dad...wasn't feeling well. Jane, you know Jane...she's coming by to pick you up. You'll be spending some time at *Honesty House*."

"That place?"

"Now don't fight me on this. It's a safe place, until I can come and get you."

"When will that be?"

Susan looked over at her husband. His breathing was shallow and the man she had grown to love with everything she possessed, was still not awake.

Her own father had died of a heart attack when she was only two. She couldn't remember that, but she would always remember this. Susan took a deep breath and touched her beloved's hand. *How long?*

Love in All its Forms

Five hours later, Henry's eyes opened. The doctors were hopeful. Still, it would be a long while before Henry would feel well again. She remembered the weeks it had taken him after his first attack. But things had been far worse then. He'd been taken from the hospital against his will and hidden away for three days before she'd found him, weak and barely alive.

She smiled at him now and touched his hand. He didn't speak but she could see the love he had for her within his eyes.

"I'm going to take care of everything," she said. "The children are with Jane."

He stared at her, his eyes burning.

"William? Well, William, thankfully, is behind bars where he belongs. I don't know what my mother's going to do about that or about the fact that I didn't send the children to her, but I don't care. All I care about is you getting well."

He blinked a tear from his eye.

"I'm sorry," she said, squeezing his hand a bit tighter. "I should have remembered your heart. We should have been more careful. It won't happen again."

He looked at her strangely and returned the grip—weak as the grip was.

Susan knew life wouldn't be easy while her husband recuperated, she was even more sure of the fact when the police found her at the hospital and asked her to return with them to police headquarters. She had to go, of course. Make them see the truth about William. Perhaps he'd killed Bob and Kate, for no more of a reason than they were getting in the way of his plans.

What were William's plans anyway, but to marry her mother and make them all crazy with worry over her? Something just didn't make sense. She saw quite clearly how angry William must have been over Bob's swindle of the house, and Kate? Maybe the baby was his and he just couldn't stand there and allow her to tell everyone the truth.

How blind she must have been months back to think Bob only cared about the snacks he could eat while lounging on the living room couch—the time he spent in front of the computer while she worked.

She'd worked hard and then some, only to return home and find him in the same place she'd left him. Only...he must have gone out after she'd left for work—found William and her sister Kate—spent time raking in the money under the table, money that she'd never personally seen. What had Bob done with it?

The questions were coming fast and furious inside her brain now and as she walked up to the front doors, her shoulders square, her chin held high, it was all Susan could do not to shake in her boots.

She sat in the room with the window, the perfect window she couldn't see out of, but someone was more than likely looking in on. And the questions were coming. About Bob. About Kate. About William. About her mother. "Did she suspect Hope had anything to do with the deaths of Bob and Kate?"

And did she think Jane Dove was involved? The question made her laugh.

The broad-shouldered police chief sat across from her. He smiled at her easily, but waited for her reply.

"Jane has nothing to do with this. Neither does my mother," she began, placing her hands firmly on the desk in front of her so they wouldn't shake. "I mean, she's my mother!"

"But what about Bob? You say you were separated from him at the time and that he'd just discovered that you'd married. He must have been pretty upset."

Her throat closed suddenly. "Yes," she whispered.

"And your mother, what was she doing?"

"Trying to take care of him, I guess."

The man stood. He was not only broad shouldered, but tall and Susan figured, could be deadly if he put his mind to it. She looked at his name badge again: Police Chief Gregson, it read.

"Was your ex a violent man?"

"No." *If the truth were known, he was actually quite the opposite, Susan thought but didn't say.*

"Why would someone want to kill him?" he asked again, because Gregson had asked her the same question at least four other times that she remembered.

"I don't know. It didn't make sense to me either for a long time. But William did have it in for him."

"Yes, that's what you said."

"Maybe he killed Bob because Bob wouldn't give any of the swindled money back."

"But you said you never saw the money."

"That's right." Susan thought of all the times she'd stressed about money when she'd been with Bob. *Where had he kept it, if there was any of it left.*

"You say your sister was connected in all of this—mess. What was her relationship with William?"

Susan breathed in and out slowly. Hadn't she already answered that question? Hadn't she already told the man that she didn't know? William could have been the father of her child, or he could have merely been—if merely was a word in this situation—someone she worked with.

"My sister must have been in love with William. At least, that's my guess. She was pregnant, but again, I'm not sure if the child was William's."

"Why do you suppose William married your mother?"

"I wish I knew. I mean, they're more naturally suited to one another—in age at least—but it does seem awful strange that William would take such a liking to my mother when he'd obviously been working, maybe even sleeping, with Kate. I don't think anyone, other than William would have a reason to kill either Bob or Kate."

"What if it was someone else?"

The thought may have crossed Susan's mind a time or two, but she hadn't ever allowed the thoughts to stay within her mind. It was funny, really, but she really believed it was all about getting William to confess to both crimes. Hadn't he had a reason to kill them both?

"Why did you have your husband's gun at the Clarition's?"

Now, here was a question. "I was cold. I'd given my coat away and Henry offered his."

"Where was your coat?"

"Clariton's wife, Chris. She had it."

"Chris. Where is she now?"

"I don't know."

Chief Gregson stood, folding his arms. "We have talked with William. He believes you were out there in search of him. That you intended to kill him."

"What?!"

"So, why were you at the Clariton's?"

"Henry and I, we were hoping to find a clue as to who murdered Bob and Kate. We were lucky and discovered that Chris was there. She told us that her husband was innocent of the crimes and that we should be looking carefully at William. What was it she said? Oh, yes. 'William can't be trusted.'"

"You said they were selling drugs and forging documents..."

"That's what she told me."

"Finding David Clariton dead was not a good omen," the police chief said, sitting down again and peering at her from across the table. "Who else should we know about?"

"Frank Olmstead, he could have done it. According to Chris, he was the mastermind behind the whole operation. And Lane Kennedy, he lived just behind Clariton."

"Yes, we know that. Anyone else?"

Susan shrugged her shoulders. "I don't know," she said. "Can I go now?"

***

"You mean to tell me that you pointed a gun at my husband with no intent to kill him?"

Her mother was raving angry. She still wore her pajamas and her hair, as in many days recently, hadn't yet been brushed. "I get a call from the police. They call me in. I see you walking out the opposite door just as I arrive. I think, 'Why is Susan here? Why am I here?' but I haven't time to think about that. I'm shoved into a small room and this man—this, this police officer breathes down my neck about my wedded husband! He's in jail, do you know that?"

Susan nodded.

"You have done this, Susan and I will never forgive you! Leave my house at once!"

Susan bowed her head. She was about to turn when she saw the white couch and thought again of the day she'd found out about Bob's death. Her husband—ex-husband forever more, wouldn't want her to give up because he hadn't given up. He had searched for her and despite his poor choices he had yet loved her enough to go in search of her. Could she do any less?

"Your husband is in jail because he killed Bob and Kate!"

A sob escaped Susan's lips. She wouldn't retain her thoughts any longer—she couldn't. "Do you know why the children are with Jane? Because I can trust her, that's why. William might have struck out against my children at any time. How could I have been sure that you would have protected them in favor of sheltering your wedded husband!"

"You are a cruel daughter!" her mother wailed. "I knew it the minute you were born!"

Susan blinked at her mother and her mouth opened but nothing came out. When the words finally revealed themselves, she screamed, "I might have a hard head, I might have married the wrong man, I might even stick my nose in places it shouldn't be, but I don't lie to myself!"

"And how am I lying, daughter? Tell me that."

"Your husband is a murderer. He may have fathered a child, your daughter's child and all you care about is saving his precious hide!"

"And why not?" she sniffed. "Why not? I love him!"

"How can you stay married to a man who is so dishonest with you?"

Hope placed her arms around her middle. "I love him, I tell you and I want you out of my house." The words were barely above a whisper, but Susan had more than heard them.

William

When Susan arrived at *Honesty House*, she reached for her children. They were in the main waiting area playing a game of Monopoly with some of the other children.

"I didn't think you'd come back," Brianne said, touching Susan's face and wiping the tears that she saw there. Susan did the same, for there were small tears on Brianne's cheeks as well. Oscar was surprised, but his tough exterior overshadowed any feelings she might have seen.

"Are you okay?" she asked them both.

"Sure. How is Dad?"

"Fine. Fine."

"Did his heart stop?" Brianne asked.

"Sort of," Susan answered. "It was in trouble. We are just going to have to be more careful with Daddy," she added, feeling guilty even as she said it. If it wasn't for her, wasn't for her carelessness in searching for clues at the Clariton's, none of this would have happened.

"Why does Daddy's heart have problems?" Brianne asked.

"Well, he was born with a too-big heart," Susan answered matter-of-factly—the child deserved that— "and it's just gotten worse over the years."

"That's why Dad has a desk job," added Oscar, looking into his sister's eyes. "If he gets his heart pumping too hard he has a heart attack. That's right, isn't it, Mom?"

Susan breathed in slowly. Her son was pretty smart—maybe even too smart. What she knew for sure was that Oscar had taken care of his sister when she and Henry couldn't be there. He'd taken them both in the house and kept his sister safe.

"Thank you for taking such good care of your sister," she said now, reaching for her son, her left arm wrapped around his waist, her right arm wrapped around the tiny waist of Brianne. "I am so glad you two knew what to do when I didn't show up at the bus stop."

"I was so scared," Brianne said. "Don't do it again."

Oscar smiled. "Mom can't promise that. But she will try very hard not to, right Mom?"

Susan nodded and looked to see Jane approach them. She was all smiles.

"So you're here!"

"I'm so sorry it took me so long. There was the hospital and then the police station..."

"What were you doing with the cops?" Oscar asked.

Susan swallowed. Like many other times in her life she had spoken first without thinking. "They just had some questions for me," she said. "Nothing to worry about."

But Oscar wasn't convinced. That night, after Brianne had been tucked into bed and she tried to sleep, Oscar entered the room. He rubbed his eyes and asked if he could sleep in her bed. When she said, no, he prodded: "Please, Mom. I have to ask you more about the interrogation."

"Where did you learn such a big word?" she asked, patting the space next to her.

"At school. So why did you have to go to the police station?"

"Your father and I are investigating."

"Investigating what?"

"Well, I told you about Bob and you know about Kate."

"I know that weird man that met us at the funeral is about as creepy as they come."

"Why do you say that?" Her son scrunched down further under the covers. It was a cold night and even with the heater on, she could feel the slight chill coming through the cracks around the window.

"I know he has something to do with this mess. Brianne and I have talked a lot about him. He was pretty strange when we first met him and even more strange at the funeral."

Susan's eyes popped open, though minutes before she had allowed the drowsiness to overtake her. "So, you met Frank in front of your old place?"

"Yeah. He was wearing a nice suit and tie—purple. It was so bright I could hardly see anything else. And then at the funeral, when we saw him again I got this strange feeling in my stomach. I talked to Brianne about it and she said she had the same thing happen to her when she saw him. What do you think it means?"

"I'm not sure," said Susan, looking her boy straight in the eye. What should she tell a 13-year-old boy? How much should he really know about what she did when he was in school? "I think maybe, we just need to watch out for him."

"So, when did you see him after the funeral? I know he wanted to meet you."

Susan blinked, then tried to feign tiredness. She rubbed her eyes and snuggled back under the covers.

"Mom. Don't. I know you saw him after the funeral."

Susan bolted upright, the blanket falling from her shoulders. "What do you mean, you know?"

"I just know, that's all. I think you've been talking to Frank and I think he's been telling you stuff. What stuff, Mom?"

It was difficult to breathe and she couldn't lie to her son, but how much should she tell him? Again, the question filtered within her brain like a single light. What did the boy need to know?

"You're right," she finally said. "And now...now that your father is in the hospital, you will need to know in case..." She stopped, because how could she go on? Could she tell her son that they were going behind the police? That they'd been doing their own thing for weeks now? Could she share the heartache she felt whenever she thought of her mother and the man she'd married? Would she ever stop grieving for Kate? And would she finally and forevermore find the answer to Bob's death?

"Mom?"

Susan reached for her son. "I guess it's about time you knew," she said.

But in the end, Susan hadn't shared everything with her son—how could she? She spoke of Frank, how she had met with him a couple of times, though she hadn't said where (why worry the boy about the man breaking into their house?) and that Frank knew something about Kate's and Bob's deaths. She spoke of his grandmother—how worried she was that she was losing her mind, how she worried that having William in jail would make things even worse in the mind of her mother. She even spoke of trying to locate clues as to why Kate had died at the Clariton's and why she thought William was involved—the man was in jail after all—it would be safe to share her heart in regards to William.

But she didn't tell her son of the possible connection to William and Kate. She didn't share with him the truth about the baby her sister had carried or the others—Lane Kennedy and Chris Clariton, who had found themselves in the middle of this mystery. There was only so much a boy of thirteen could take in.

***

Jane was frantic. "The wedding! I need your help!"

Susan was alone in the house, though she'd decided to spend some time working on the clues to the double murder. Heads were hard to crack, but easier, once everything was put to paper. She was just spreading out the names and situations on the kitchen table when her cell phone rang.

"The wedding is only a month away and I have far too much to do. Can you come by for a few days and take over while I go shopping? I haven't had time."

Jane's voice was stilted and far from kind, but Susan knew what it felt like to be up against a deadline—though her own wedding must have been simple in its implementation the way Jane was carrying on.

"Sure, I'd love to help," she said, looking down at the scraps of paper that would have to be shelved for another day. She began to gather them when there was a knock at the door. "Just a sec." Placing the remaining pieces of paper in an envelope and laying the envelope on the table, she walked to the door.

"Mother."

"That's right. Can I come in?"

"Sure...Jane? I'll be over in a bit. Will that work?"

An audible sigh drifted into the receiver. "Thank you, Susan."

Susan watched her mother enter the room. She wore a striking silver dress though it was morning and had braided her silver-red hair in coils on the top of her head. Pulling off her gloves, she sat. She was wearing matching shoes today—the snow had melted, at least for the time being.

"I've just gone to visit William," she began, wiping a stray tear from her eye. Susan noticed that they were bloodshot; her lips trembled as she spoke. "He told me that if I wanted any questions answered I needed to talk with you."

Susan sat down uneasily. She pushed the envelope to the side of the table. "What do you want to know?" she asked.

"Why is my husband really in jail?"

"What do you mean?"

"Why is he in jail? You held the gun. You should be in a jail!"

"Mother...I..."

"I can't believe what you've done to Bob, to Kate and now to my dear William!" She sobbed into her hands and for moments that Susan dared not calculate, she watched the tears dripping between her mother's fingers. Had she been so cruel as to make life miserable for her own mother? No. She'd merely tried to find the killer of Bob and her sister Kate. And now David Clariton was dead, though she cared little for his life other than the fact that his wife, Chris was heartbroken.

What could she possibly say?

As her mother cried, the tears continuing to fall, Susan stood and walked to the kitchen stove. "Let me make you some tea," she said, reaching for a cup. "It will help."

She could feel her mother's red eyes on her back even before she turned. "Nothing will help! My love is gone! He is trapped in that jail cell until he reveals everything! His involvement with Bob, his leanings toward Kate. Why...he went to the Clariton home that day you held a gun to him! That David Clariton, did you know he's dead? Did you also know that that Frank person—and that Lane...what is his name...Kennedy, is traipsing around the area, too?"

Susan's mother was sobbing now, her shoulders rising and falling with each breath. "I don't know what to do!"

Susan turned from her mother and began to fill the teapot. She placed the pot on the stove and turned on the burner. When she turned to say something to her mother, she was no longer at the table but behind the counter, her glittering fingernails splayed out like a spider's tentacles.

"Tell me everything. Now."

If Susan lived to be a million years old she would never forget what happened next. As her mother stood at her counter, tears spilling down her cheeks like thundering rain, she spoke about William and all she believed about him—including that he had been the father of Kate's unborn child.

Henry

Jane ran to Susan when she saw her. "I can't believe it! You're here!"

Actually, Susan was glad to be at *Honesty House*, though it had taken her almost two hours to pull herself away from her mother. This she explained to Jane only to have the woman flutter her hands in excitement.

"Conrad will be here tonight! He's taking me out to dinner!"

"Conrad?"

"My fiancé'!" The woman was giddy with excitement. "Can you stay until two or so? I know you have kids to pick up, but I'll need some time to get things in order. I still have to order the cake and all the linens!"

Susan smiled. "So, it's Conrad, huh?" In all of the excitement of living her own life and allowing Jane to take care of *Honesty House*, there hadn't been much talk about the man she was going to marry—surprisingly, including his name—or had she told her and she'd forgotten? "Sure. You go and do your thing. I'll see you soon, okay?"

Jane blinked back a tear. "I can hardly believe it."

Susan couldn't either. Besides a few facts about that man, that he traveled a lot and spent as much time with Jane as possible, she knew little about the man who was to become her best friend's husband. Well, she would have to change that.

"Sometime soon, maybe before this wedding excitement is all over, you'll have time to introduce me to him," she said.

"Oh! I'm so sorry. Yes, let's do that." She turned and grabbed her coat and purse. "I've got to go!"

Susan watched the woman she had known for months now, the woman who almost singlehandedly had kept the roof on and the children happy within the walls of *Honesty House*. And when Jane was no longer in eyesight, she turned to the children gathering at her feet.

***

Henry was awake. He smiled at her weakly from his hospital bed and motioned her closer. It had been a week since his attack, an attack the doctors were now saying would make blood clots even more a reality if he didn't take care of himself. A blood clot had caused his last heart attack—fortunately, the clot hadn't traveled to his lungs—a sure sign of pulmonary embolism.

"So, you've decided to finally come and visit me," he said wearily, trying to sit up. Though her husband still looked pale, he did smile and that old twinkle in his eye had returned.

"Let me fix your hair," she said, taking a comb from her purse and parting his red hair down the middle. "There, that's better," she said once finished.

"Thanks, Mom." He smiled over at her again and reached for her hand. "I can't believe I'm still here."

"I can." She thought about the terrible events that had preceded his hospital stay. The bad news was that William was no longer in jail because there hadn't been anything to really pin him on. After a full 72-hours, he hadn't been charged with anything and had been sent home.

She worried about her mother, wondered if she'd be safe. If they'd all be safe.

"How are the kids?" he asked.

She propped a pillow under his head. "Good. They miss you."

"I miss them, too. You know, I never really thought I could be a dad, but having those two running around and causing trouble has sure made my life interesting."

"You could say that." She smiled down at him a squeezed his hand.

"I hope my heart heals sufficiently, if you know what I mean."

For a minute she didn't and then a new smile creased her face. 'Is that all you can think about?"

He smiled back at her a pulled her to him. When they kissed she couldn't help but think of all the love she held for him; this man who had brought her a cup of sugar so long ago and had bothered her to no end to date him.

"So, how is the sleuthing coming?" he asked.

"How soon until you can get out of here?" she countered.

"Any day now. I've had more exams than I'd like to count, more blood tests than I'd like to remember and more hospital food than I'd care to mention."

"I'm glad they're not going to have to operate," she said, though Susan was well aware that operating had been considered—and why her husband was still in the hospital when most patients would have been released much sooner. "And I'm sorry I haven't been here 24/7," she added, with just a touch of regret.

"What, leave the children with Jane the entire time? Your mother would have had a fit!"

She laughed. "Speaking of Mother. She came to the house and we talked. She is pretty angry at me."

"Because the kids..."

She waved the comment away. "No, she thinks I've caused all of the problems between her and William. I don't think my mother is thinking straight."

"When I get out of this bed, we'll talk to her together," said Henry, closing his eyes briefly and then opening them again. "Where's William?"

She almost hated telling him. But she did anyway. She didn't want him to worry, but most of all she didn't want to be the cause of another heart attack.

***

The following day, Henry came home, but he was weak. The children, once off to school, gave her and Henry some time to talk. Henry wanted to know all about what he'd been missing. And she told him, as calmly and truthfully as possible. But it wasn't easy.

William was back home, though she hadn't heard yet from her mother—if that was actually a good thing, though she was sure her mother had taken him in with open arms. Frank Olmstead hadn't been seen recently and Lane Kennedy—who knows where that man was—he hadn't returned to his home, at least not that she knew.

Jane was so in love and there was so much to do, that Susan had finally relented for a few more fill-ins at *Honesty House* so her friend could get the wedding preparations handled. Chris, David's widow, hadn't been seen either, at least, that's what the police had finally told her when she'd called.

Henry got up and shaved and when he returned to her she was almost finished preparing breakfast. "Sit down for a little something," she said, placing some eggs and bacon on a plate.

"Thanks," he offered, taking a bite. He finished what was on his plate and then waved her over to the table.

"I've missed you something fierce," he said.

"Now, remember what the doctor said."

"I know. But after such a fine breakfast I have plenty of energy." He winked at her.

"Can we wait? I mean, this is the first day that you've been home."

"I guess. If that's what you really want."

She peered over her eggs, or what was left of them, and smiled.

***

"Daddy!" Brianne squealed, tossing herself on the bed where Henry had been sleeping. He opened his eyes and peered over at her.

"I see you've returned from school," he said. "Did you have a good day?"

"I drew this!" She reached into her backpack and pulled out a painting. It was of a man in a dark suit and two children standing at his feet.

"Is that me?"

"Of course not, silly! It's that bad man, Frank."

"And the little..."

"Me and brother. Can't you tell?"

Actually, he could. He could also see the shack in the distance and the purple tie at the man's throat. "Why would you want to draw Frank?" he asked, sitting up.

"He needs to be put in jail," was Brianne's answer. "He's a bad man."

"How do you know he's a bad man?"

"Grandma says so."

"Oh?"

"She says that Mother is over her head." She sat on the bed and reached for him. "I missed you so much, Daddy!"

Hugging Brianne was like hugging love to the fullest. "I love you, too," he said, looking up in just that moment. Susan was standing in the doorway.

"So, you're the one who woke Daddy up," she said.

The girl smiled mischievously at her. "Yep, it was me."

"Well, *me*, take yourself to your room and hang up your backpack. I need to talk to your daddy alone for a minute."

Brianne hopped off the bed, her long legs dancing to her bedroom.

"So, what do you think?" he asked, showing Susan the picture.

"I don't know what to think, but I know one thing for sure. We need to get to my mother's."

A Visitor

February was only two weeks away by the time Susan felt like Henry was well enough to travel with her to her mother's. Sure, she was an old mother hen making him wait an additional week to see her, besides the fact that they needed to get through Christmas and New Year's, but the wait just had to be.

This year had been special—but with two great kids how could the holidays have been anything else. She had seen her mother during that time and William, briefly, as he'd walked by her to the kitchen for something to drink. But she had said nothing at that time and he'd said nothing either.

And so, the holidays had gone by without a hitch. Frank and his compatriots were nowhere to be found as far as she knew and Jane Dove was finishing up her wedding plans, though Susan had not yet met Conrad Jackson.

"So, what's up with your fiancé'? she finally asked her friend moments before Jane took off for another wedding errand. It was wedding shoes today—shoes she hadn't been able to find.

"Up?"

"You know. I haven't met him yet."

She smiled. "On another business trip. I won't even see him myself until the day before the wedding."

"What?"

"It's painful, I know. But at least this way I can get the shopping done without being distracted." Jane blushed.

"Really, Jane."

Jane pulled on her coat. "Same time? Or do you need to be back sooner for your husband?"

"No. He's up and getting around great now. In fact, he's willing to come and start here as soon as you need him. I won't even have to fill in."

Jane's jaw dropped. She buttoned her coat. "Okay, well then, I'll see you soon, alright?"

***

As it turned out, Jane was late and so she called Henry. "Pick up the kids, will you? I'm going to be working late."

"Is everything alright?"

It was nearing 4 p.m. and her friend still wasn't there. "I think so," she replied.

"I'll get the kids and we'll come over and visit you."

"Are you sure?"

"You have been my mother for far too long. Besides, I need to get out. I was thinking to start at *Honesty House* on Monday. When Jane gets there, we can bawl her out for being late and then I can tell her the good news." Susan could feel the smile from Henry's lips. The last thing on Henry's mind would be to upset anyone, but she wondered, quite suddenly, how Jane would react once she heard Henry's news.

Jane arrived a half an hour later and she wasn't happy. She rushed to the desk in a crying fury. "Are your kids alright? I'm so sorry I wasn't here!" As she pulled off her coat, Susan noticed a distinct red mark across her cheek.

"Conrad, is he back?" she couldn't help asking.

"Oh, no, no. I need to sit." Jane reached for a chair behind the main desk. "You won't believe what happened. I was accosted!"

"What?"

Henry drew near and it was if Jane was seeing him and the children for the first time. "Oh," she said. "I'm glad everyone is alright."

"Couldn't be better. Who struck you?" Henry asked.

Brianne huddled around Susan, Oscar was nowhere in sight. "Find your brother," she said.

Brianne blinked up at her. "What's wrong with Jane?" she asked.

Jane smiled down at the child. "Go and find your brother and then come and tell me," she offered.

That seemed to satisfy the girl. In moments, she'd gone to retrieve her brother.

"Thanks," Susan offered. "What happened?"

"I was at that great shop, you know the one—Corianne's on Fifth?"

When Susan nodded, Jane continued: "I was trying on the perfect pair of shoes when this woman walked up to me. Quite rudely she said, "You can't marry him. You can't marry Conrad Jackson."

"Who was this woman? Do we know her?"

"I don't think so. She was dressed as if she had nowhere to go. Probably homeless."

"Drunk, more than likely," Henry offered.

"That's what I thought, too, at least at first." And here Jane breathed in deeply and wiped her eyes where tears had begun to form. "She seemed to know all about me, that I ran *Honesty House*, that I took in children. She was 'afraid for them, too' she said. And she knew you, Susan. I couldn't believe it myself at first, but when she kept talking, I realized she knew more than she should."

"What did this woman look like?" Henry asked.

Stringy hair. A dirty blue blouse. I think her hair was blond but it was hard to tell. After she slapped me for not believing her, she said her name was Chris."

***

Susan couldn't believe it. Neither could Henry. Chris knew Conrad.

"Have you ever met Jane's fiancé?" she asked, pretty sure he hadn't.

"No, but I figured you had."

When Susan shook her head, Henry dialed the police department. "I need to come in and soon," he said. "Want to come with?" he asked when he'd finished.

"Sure but..." She'd been thinking about her mother all morning. Wondering what William was doing—saying, now that he was no longer being held for questioning. Besides, what would she do with the children?

He seemed to guess at her uneasiness. "We'll only be gone a short time, let's ask Oscar."

"Oscar?"

"You told me yourself that Oscar took pretty good care of his sister when we didn't show up to pick them up and it sounds like both of them have handled your mother pretty well. We haven't seen Olmstead for weeks now. I don't think he'll be coming back."

"But are you sure? I really don't feel comfortable leaving them."

"I can do it." Oscar's sudden voice in the hallway made Susan and Henry turn. "You need to find the killer."

Brianne peeked around the doorframe. "Oscar can watch me," she said.

In the end, her heart still beating like a band drum, she'd left them. Perhaps it was time to do a bit more trusting and live her life with a bit less—fear. She thought of her mother again, living with a man Susan wondered how she could trust. Well, she had a good man and a good son and daughter. What was there to worry about?

Still, as she and Henry backed from the driveway, Susan took one more glance at the house and prayed that everything would be alright.

***

When they returned, the children were in bed. "See, what did I tell you?" said Henry. "The best news is that our children are safe and that the police are looking into this Conrad Jackson."

"Yes, and upping the chase for Chris Clariton. Where do you suppose she is? And why would she care to contact Jane?"

"She knows this Conrad character and perhaps he's no good as she says," replied Henry, grabbing his pajamas and putting them on.

"If you're right, we need to talk with Jane. We probably should have already talked to her."

"It's late. Tomorrow will be soon enough." He tapped the bed with the palm of his hand.

***

Her mother was angry. No surprise there. At first she wouldn't even open the door. William glared above her. He was wearing a white shirt, pressed. His khaki pants were perfectly creased.

"I think you've hurt your mother enough," the man began, placing a hand on Hope's shoulder. She reached up with her own and covered it.

"William's right. You'd better go."

"But are you all right, Mother? Has William hurt you?"

Her mother's mouth opened to speak and then she clamped it tight, the fine lines on her painted lips narrowing.

"You'd better go," William repeated.

"Wait!" Henry's foot reached for the door that was quickly being closed.

Hope looked down.

"Susan is just concerned. Don't you want to find out who killed Bob? Who took Kate's life?"

William smiled. "Of course we do," he said, "but we are waiting on the police. What can you two possibly do?"

"Oh, I don't know, William. Did you ever tell the police why you were at the Clariton place?"

Susan was suddenly cold. She wrapped her coat—a new one Henry had purchased for her since Chris had her old one—around her body. But it was no use. The wind was bitter.

"Who are the Clariton's?" Hope asked, turning to her husband.

"Just some old...friends," was his answer. He proceeded to direct his wife from the door.

As the door shut, Susan turned to Henry. "It's no use," she said. "William's got my mother wrapped around his little finger. She wouldn't see the truth if it hit her in the face."

Henry knocked on the closed door. After a few moments, William returned—alone. "I told you to leave," he said.

"Not until we get some questions answered," replied Henry. "Can we come in? Susan is cold..."

"Like I said, we've had enough of your hysterics. Your mother is down for a nap."

"Who is Conrad Jackson?" Henry asked.

There was a momentary flinch, almost imperceptible, but Susan had seen it. Had Henry?

"Who?" William asked. He peered out the front door.

"Conrad Jackson. Evidently Chris Clariton knows him, too."
William's skin paled. "I've got to go," he said.

"Let us in!" Susan hadn't meant it to be a wail, but there it was. "What are you afraid of?"

William blinked and the door widened. "Nothing," he said, "nothing at all."

After Susan had checked up on her mother and found that she was sleeping as William had told them, she sat next to Henry on the white couch that had begun this mess. Bob had died here and her sister, Kate, had been sitting in this very room. Now she was gone. Would be forever...gone.

"I suppose I need to tell you about the second note," Susan began, patting Henry's hand as if asking for support. But he always gave it—always.

"What note?" William asked, crossing his legs and staring into her eyes. What did she see there? Was it worry? Stress? A combination of guilt and concern for the woman he'd married? Was he still trying with everything he had to cover up what he'd done? What?

"I should have told you. Here." She placed the wrinkled note into William's hands.

Lifting the note, he began to read. "Sounds like a going away letter," he finally said, bringing the note up to the light as if he were looking for signs of a fake bill.

"Did Mother tell you she found the note behind the couch?"
William shook his head. "No."

"I think this is the first note that Bob penned. Maybe he thought it was too soft or something and that's why he wrote out the other note that Mother found after he was dead."

"Your mother didn't find it," said William, placing his palms on his slacks. "Kate did. And she was pretty upset, too. Couldn't calm her down."

"What?"

"Why should that matter? The note was found, that's all that's important."

Susan thought of her sister and how she'd missed her these last few months. She thought about her perfectionism, all of the things that had caused her personal grief. Susan remembered their fine talks, especially after Kate had come to live with her. She remembered the ache in her sister's heart about the baby she was carrying and how

William wouldn't step up to his responsibilities. Was it really true that he was the father?

"Bob didn't commit suicide."

"And Kate? You think I killed her, don't you?"

Henry squirmed uneasily next to her. "Well, did you?"

"I need to be honest, it's the least I can do since causing all of that trouble at the Clariton place."

Susan waited in anticipation.

William stood and walked to the frosted window. The frost would probably continue for at least another month, before the warmth of spring hit the area. Oh, how Susan was dreaming for spring.

"I thought about killing her, you have to know that. I went to the Clariton place, that first time, hoping to see her, to talk to her about the mess she'd caused me and your mother. But when I got there, Kate was already gone. I found her out back. No one was there and I just left her."

"What?" Susan sobbed.

"I couldn't be implicated; can't you see that?" The man wrung his hands and turning to them, placed them inside his pant pockets. "Your sister, she's...she tried to get me to admit that I was the father. At least at first. When she knew I wouldn't cave, she threatened me with my life."

"I...I left her and found your mother. I couldn't believe a woman could love me so much. She knew some of my past, though I never shared with her that I knew Kate. I can only imagine what would have happened if I had."

Susan was filled with disbelief. "You mean to tell me that this was all Kate's doing?"

"Yes. When you saw me at Kennedy's, I was searching as you were, for clues. I want to find the killer as much, perhaps even more so, than you do."

"That's highly impossible," Henry said now, taking Susan by the hand and giving it a short squeeze. "Kate was Susan's sister."

William returned to his chair and sat down. "I don't expect you to understand," he said, wiping his hands on his pants and looking away to the window. "The police are so close to finding out the truth, I just can't be a part of their findings. I will do anything..."

His voice trailed off and when he looked up, tears were forming in his eyes. "Believe me when I say that I didn't kill your sister. I didn't kill Bob. All I want is to completely clear my name and get on with my life with your mother."

"So, what is the truth?" Henry asked, leaving Susan for a moment and sitting in the chair across from William. "Tell us."

"I don't know if I can..." the man sobbed into his hands.

Susan was beyond belief. This man, who had always held it together, was breaking down before their very eyes! Like her mother, who was not the same, hadn't been the same since she'd begun to learn the truth of her husband—this man was finally ready to share it all.

"Bob had it in for me since the beginning. You know about the house I never received. That was all the money I had in the world. When he got off—scot free—and I had to suffer in jail, I was so angry, I could have gotten out of jail and come to kill him. And he would have deserved it. I'd lost my job and a young girl, way too young for me, was telling me I was the father of her child. I just had to escape!" He laughed then, wiping the tears from his cheeks.

"I ran crazily into the arms of your mother and she let me, bless her heart. Atheist or no atheist, she loved me. I couldn't understand it. The first few weeks, before Bob came to live with us, were pure bliss. But I was in for another shock when he arrived. I knew Bob. I was enmeshed in a terrible dilemma."

"I would say so," Susan smiled. "And Kate just happened to see you in the garage with a bit of Gatorade."

He looked over at her. "That," he said lamely, "was a mistake."

"I should think so," said Henry.

"A shouldn't have even thought it," said William.

"You know what the Bible says," interjected a smirking Henry. William blinked.

If William had been thinking it, there was a good chance he could have followed through with the act, Susan thought. But had he? Looking on William now, she couldn't help but wonder. Sure, he was rude and he seemed to be in the wrong places at the wrong times, but killing Bob because he'd been swindled out of money, and her sister, because she'd said he was the father of her child, did that really give him a heavy enough reason to murder?

Perhaps for some, Susan reasoned, but would it be enough for William?

"So I've had money problems and...women problems." He looked over at Susan, but I would never kill anyone, you have to believe me. After Bob was found murdered, I did all I could to find the perpetrator even though they believed he'd committed suicide. I told them about all of our conversations, all of the heated arguments. But I never hit him and I never killed him. When it came to Kate..." He sniffed before continuing, wiping his nose with a tissue from his back pocket—"She was a nice gal, but it was just my luck that she wanted more. Just my luck." He wiped at his eyes and looked directly into Susan's. "I did not kill your sister."

A dark sensation caressed Susan's back and for the first time since she'd met William she almost believed him. There was really no evidence that he hadn't killed either one of them, but she wanted to believe...

Henry took her hand. "So, who do you think did it?" he asked.

William wiped his face one last time with the handkerchief and placed the soiled material in his back pocket. "Lane Kennedy."

Susan couldn't have been more surprised, though the man's name was on the list of suspects. Along with William there was Frank Olmstead, Lane Kennedy and Chris Clariton, though Susan highly doubted the woman had the strength and wisdom to do such a thing. And she probably wouldn't kill her husband, even though he'd left her to fare life alone.

Who else? Well, there was her mother, Hope. It was the first time that she'd considered her mother as one of the suspects, but her very strange behavior, especially in recent weeks, had made her wonder if her mother was thinking normally. Would she kill Bob and then break down because of it? Would she kill her own daughter because she had turned out to be less than perfect?

The thought of it made Susan's skin crawl and yet the thought of it remained.

The most penetrating question yet remained, however. Bob had been poisoned in her mother's living room. Kate had been poisoned at the Clariton residence. Two murders had taken place. And if two murders, perhaps *two* suspects.

Henry let go of her hand. In its place was clamminess. So, she wasn't the only one worried about finding out the truth. "So, what you're telling us," Henry began, "is that Lane Kennedy has spearheaded this whole thing."

"I just said Kennedy was the killer," William said.

Susan's heart stopped. What could William possibly mean?

"There are many sharks in the ocean and not all of the sharks are swimming in the water." William peered up at them from his sitting position. "Have you ever considered that there might be someone else, someone still incarcerated who is pulling the strings?"

"Like who?" Susan asked.

"Think about it. Who hated you more than life itself when you put him in jail?"

"I didn't put anyone in jail."

William stood, wringing his hands. He reached around back and grabbed the soiled tissue from his back pocket. Dabbing at his nose, he continued: "Who's in prison thirty years to life?"

Susan's mind reeled. Well, there was Carter Childs. She remembered his anger, but he seemed to take the verdict in stride; it was Ephraim Humphrey, brother-in-law to Lane Kennedy who had taken the news especially hard. She still remembered the man's dark eyes, taking her in. It couldn't be him, could it?

And if so, who would he direct to do his dirty work? The thought just made her sick, but it had to be true. Ephraim Humphrey might just be directing someone on the outside. And if so, who?

Her eyes turned again to William. He was there when Bob had died and he knew exactly where to look for David Clariton. He could have easily killed Kate.

"I can't help it...I..." Susan began.

"I know what you're thinking, but I tell you again, I'm not your man. The killer could even be a woman for all I know."

Wedded Bliss?

Susan watched Henry from the corner of her eye. Did the man look sad? Even as he directed the troop, the boys and girls who made their way to *Honesty House* for a place to sleep, a place to eat or a place to feel at home, she wondered.

Though his eyes lit up every time a child came to him and tugged on his pant leg, or asked him a question, or even cried for some comforting, life just wasn't the same for a man used to the hard-pressed days of sleuthing. At every turn there was risk, at any moment a secret would be discovered, a way out manifested. But not here. And it seemed to Susan that her husband would never be the same until he went back to police business.

She tried not to let it bother her, but each day as he left for work, there was a sorrowful look in Henry's eyes, sorrow that hadn't been there before and so today she'd offered to come with him, just to help out a little and he'd relented—besides, it would only be while, their children were in school.

Jane was on another shopping trip for the wedding. The dress purchased, the shoes held secretly within the bottom of the zippered bag, all her friend had left was to finalize the food. Susan sat at the welcoming desk as her husband went about directing Mrs. Grimble about the cooking—the third cook they'd hired since *Honesty House's* opening. For all Ms. Pratt had had with all of her complaining and the short visit her sister had given them before her death, Mrs. Grimble was a fascinating cook and down and out—organized.

Mr. Gobel, the grounds keeper, spent most of his time indoors since the change of weather, but he was known to walk the grounds on a daily basis to clear the walks and check on the trees and frozen plant life.

The girls, Miranda and Chelsea, were still moving forward famously. They cleaned the rooms and spent their days playing and helping out with the children in the main room.

Still, all was not right with her husband and Susan wasn't sure what she could possibly do about it.

Upon Jane's return, with smiles that continued and had no end, Susan asked if there was anything specific she could help with the wedding.

The woman's eyes lit up. "Of course! Can you help me decorate this place and set up the tables? The food will be catered, but I'm doing the rest."

"Sure, I'd be glad to," was the only reply worth giving. Jane Dove was her best friend after all. Jane had opted out of the typical bridal line after the ceremony, preferring a less formal party feel, which was fine with Susan who didn't like others gaping at her anyway. She could help her friend without the staring looks.

As the day wore on to late afternoon, Susan found her husband and told him she was leaving to get the children. "I'll see you tonight," she said. But the words seemed hollow as he responded with a smile that seemed more pasted on than real.

Susan gathered up her supplies, her coat, everything she'd brought with her, said her good-byes to Jane and left *Honesty House*. Her car was parked out back—away from the crowds that sometimes made their way up to the front entrance. She thought about Henry again and then the children, her last thoughts on Jane Dove. Only days from now she'd be sharing her wedding vows with a man Susan had never met. Susan hoped he was a good man and would treat her friend well. She hoped her friend would be happy and that, after all, she'd be able to see her even though Jane would no longer be working at *Honesty House*

She wondered, too, if she should share these foreboding feelings with Jane and if so, how Jane would react to them. That she'd never met Jane's fiancé meant nothing, not really. Jane was a grown woman with a good head on her shoulders. Still, something nagged at her, something Susan just couldn't explain.

Gathering her coat closer around her she reached for the key lock. Just a few weeks past, the battery operated door opening on her key fob had stopped working—now she'd have to do things the old fashioned way.

The key slid into the lock and turning it, she opened the door and slid in, but not before something reached for her. She didn't see it at first, just felt the hand as it clasped against her mouth, pushing her inside and following its way behind her. The door slammed shut. She was on the hump between the passenger's seat and the driver's.

She wanted to scream, but the cold hand was pressed even more strongly against her mouth. It pushed her passed the brake and to the passenger side. Susan's head clanked against the window. Touching her head, she turned to see Chris Clariton staring at her.

"Where's your keys?" she demanded.

Susan held them out like a talisman. "Here," she said.

The woman started the ignition, then looking at her only once, barked, "You'd better get your seat belt on. It's going to be some ride." She smiled, but the smile was pasted on, almost like the smile Henry had glued on when she'd left him. Only with Chris, there was something glaringly wrong in her eyes.

Susan snapped on the seatbelt and stared at Chris. Was this the same woman who'd appeared innocent at their first meeting?

The car lurched from its parking position and Chris maneuvered it forward to the first turn.

"I have to get my children," Susan said. "They'll be waiting." The thought of leaving them again, not arriving as she'd told them, gave her far too many memories she hoped to have forgotten. But then again, did she want Chris to pick up her children? She wished she hadn't said anything.

"You've given them a house key," she said. "They'll be alright."

Susan wondered how Chris knew that her children had a house key, but maybe all children were given a house key and so the woman was just trying to calm her nerves.

"We need to talk." She drove past the bus stop where Brianne and Oscar would be dropped off and was glad they weren't there yet—waiting. She prayed that Oscar would remember what to do—that they'd be alright as before.

Chris drove for another fifteen minutes, passing the place where she shopped and the gym where Henry exercised. The new plan would keep his heart 'strong' the doctor had told her, though all she could think about now was getting out of there, somehow, and getting to her children. As the car sped through blocks of places she knew like the back of her hand, she knew that jumping out would probably be the worst possible choice—especially at this speed.

Where was Chris taking her?

"I'm sorry I had to do this," Chris said suddenly, blinking at her briefly, then turning her face to the road. "It won't be long now."

When the car finally stopped at a light just outside of town, Susan tried the door. "I wouldn't do that if I were you," the woman said. For the first time Susan noticed that Chris was clean. Her blond hair was washed and she was wearing a new coat—not Susan's. "I'm going to stop by this old church, see it on the corner?"

When Susan nodded, letting go of the handle, the woman smiled again. "You're smart," she said. "When we're at the church, we'll talk."

Susan nodded, wondering how smart she *really* was. Her phone was in her purse, wherever that was. Being pushed into the car and then knocked in the head by a window, hadn't helped her in the search and rescue department.

She looked now, surveying the floor, the seat next to her. Nothing.

"If you're looking for your purse, you won't find it," Chris said.

Susan looked out the window and watched as Chris pulled the car into the church parking lot. Once stopped, she turned off the ignition. "It will get cold in here soon enough," she said.

The comment was strange.

"Now, you need to listen. I tried to reach you earlier—before your friend began making wedding plans but it just wasn't possible. Frank, he's watching my every move. I could have been killed just now trying to get to you." She paused and looked through the quickly steaming window.

"Lane, he's on the trail, too. My sweet David is dead and they're all after me—and you."

"Why?"

Chris laughed, but it was a sickly laugh, almost as if she were drugged or something. Her eyes pierced Susan's. She reached for her hand, grabbing it and pushing her flesh together. "Now, you listen, Susan. And you listen good."

"Let go of my hand," Susan said. The tightening was painful.

"You need to know that you're not safe, not any of you."

"What—what do you mean?"

"All of you. At the wedding. Your friend must not marry...Conrad."

"That's the most ridiculous..." she began and then she remembered how Chris had found Jane and had warned her about the same thing.

"Listen. Frank wanted you to listen, remember? He wanted to scare you, make you stop looking. No good will come of it. He...he is coming for all of us, don't you see? It was Bob first and then your sister. I'm sorry about your sister, I loved her too. And then my David. But he isn't finished. Your friend cannot marry Conrad Jackson."

Her grip released itself and Susan massaged her hand, but she did not look away from Chris' eyes. "Why can't Jane marry Conrad?"

Tears filled Chris' eyes. "You wouldn't believe me if I told you," she said, turning again to the completely fogged window. It was steadily getting colder in the car and Susan's face was losing its warmth. When Chris turned from the window there was nothing but pain on her face. "You must trust me," she said.

Chris started the ignition. Susan had no idea what time it was—her car clock had stopped working last year and she'd been thinking about fixing it along with the car beeper. Her cell phone was who knows where and the woman—a woman she'd thought would never be able to hurt a fly—was driving her back in the direction they had come.

Chris was silent as she left her in the car, the keys still in the ignition, the car running, but when she was clearly out of sight Susan reached for her purse in the back seat, turned off the ignition and with shaking hands, went in to see her husband. He was at the front desk when she walked in and with him, the children.

"Thank God!" Henry wailed.

She ran to him, embracing them all.

"Where have you been?"

She bent down. Tears fell from Brianne's small face and Oscar was hovering over her, his arm wrapped protectively around his sister's shoulders. "You did it again, Mom," he said. "We were worried."

Susan wiped the tears which had accumulated on her face. "I'm sorry," she said, "something has happened."

"What?" Oscar asked.

"I...I mean, we'll talk about it later." She looked up at Henry.

"Listen to your mother," Henry said.

Jane was suddenly around the corner. She stopped when she saw Susan. "Oh, I'm so glad. We almost called the police!"

"What time is it?" Susan asked, looking up. The clock above her read 5:15.

***

"She what?" Henry was pacing the living room. The children were finally in bed—the antics of the afternoon had kept them up until almost 11 p.m.

"She believes something terrible is going to happen at Jane's wedding. And this terrible thing has to do with Conrad."

Henry continued to pace and as Susan watched the man she loved walk back and forth, back and forth between the kitchen and living room, she finally asked it, the question that had been plaguing her mind for weeks, though she hadn't said anything to Henry.

"This Conrad, who is he really? I mean, if he's as terrible as Chris says, he's got to be connected with the three murders, right? What would she care about Jane marrying some guy that she didn't like?"

"Chris must know this Conrad. Met him somewhere. Have you met him yet?"

Susan tried to swallow. "No, it's never really worked out. "He's either out of town or the night doesn't work for some other reason."

"I find that strange and revealing."

Susan wiped her dry mouth with her fingers. "Want a drink?" she asked.

He followed her into the kitchen where she poured two sodas. They sat at the kitchen table and Susan retrieved the notes she'd written on pieces of paper and placed within the manila envelope.

Spreading out the notes, she and Henry began to read them.

"I don't see anything about Conrad," he said finally.

"I know."

"And I don't see anything here that we haven't already discussed," he added, looking down at the small pile he'd created in front of him. "William has always been a suspect and so has Frank Olmstead and Lane Kennedy. David Clariton was a suspect until he was murdered, along with Kate...I know she's not on your list, but she was on mine."

"Henry!"

"Well, I had to think of everyone. Look, you have your mother's name written down," he said, pointing.

Susan was embarrassed.

"So, why do you think your mother did it?"

"I don't know. Maybe because she's turned a little crazy. I don't think she killed Kate, of course, but Bob, she might have murdered him."

"You think so, Christian woman that she is?"

Susan sighed. "Oh, I don't know, I'm just basing my suspect list on her mind recently. She's always been a bit, you know, eccentric, but never like this."

"So, if she killed Bob, what would have been her motive?"

"Remember I lived with Bob for a long time. He wasn't the easiest man to live with."

"But killing him..."

"I know what you're saying. The thought is really out there."

"Almost like a spaceship," Henry said, smiling.

"Well, what if there were two murderers and not just one, with similar motives?"

"Give me an example."

"Oh, I don't know. Bob was a difficult person to be with. What if my mother quickly tired of Bob, especially after she found out I'd married. Maybe he wouldn't leave the house or something. And what if William had something to do with Kate's death. He did hold a huge grudge against her for the lie she'd told about him. People are hard to live with, especially a family with hard heads."

Henry laughed. The noise was good to hear. "But what about what Chris Clariton told you about the murders? This man, Conrad Jackson, perhaps he's the mastermind behind this whole thing, perhaps he's connected somehow to all three murders. And here's a thought, out there like that alien spaceship. What if Bob wasn't poisoned in your mother's living room?"

"What?"

"Suppose he was drugged before he returned home and sat on your mother's couch?"

"But he was always at home—he never went anywhere."

"But what if, that day, he went somewhere? What if we're not hearing the complete truth for some reason? What if the murder was planted at your mother's home to get someone else in trouble."

"Like who, William?"

"That's just what I'm thinking."

***

The day following, Susan made her way to *Honesty House.* Jane was pleased to see her but Susan wondered how long the excitement would last. The news on the early morning broadcast on her way to work had not been good. Chris was dead. Murdered! And probably only a few hours after visiting with her.

After sharing the news with Jane, Jane frowned.

"I can't believe it," she began. "I know the woman was strange, telling me all sorts of unbelievable things about my betrothed, but she was sort of...kind."

Susan remembered the slap but remained silent. "So what did she tell you?"

"Just as I explained. That I shouldn't marry Conrad. She was pretty insistent that I break our engagement. She said she was afraid for my life."

"You didn't tell me that before."

"I must have forgotten because of the scare. Anyway, the woman was obviously deranged or something."

The children were busy playing and Henry and the others working at *Honesty House*, other than her friend, were at least a few feet away. Still, she would have to speak softly in order not to be heard.

"Before she was killed, Chris talked with me."

"Chris?"

"The woman who came to you."

"You knew her?"

"A little bit, but you need to listen." She sounded a bit like Chris and a bit like Frank Olmstead, but she didn't care. Something was obviously—wrong.

"I'm listening." Jane leaned in.

"I don't think you should marry Conrad either," she began, "not until this entire murder investigation is solved."

Jane sat bolt upright. "You can't be serious!"

"I'm dead...serious," Susan offered. "What if Conrad Jackson isn't who he says he is? What if he's mixed up in these murders..."

"Conrad isn't even from around here. And besides, he's a good, kind man." She stood.

"I've got a lot to do."

"Please sit. Please."

Jane glared at her. "I don't know what you're thinking, Susan. I love this man."

"I know, I know. Just sit."

Jane sat, but in her eyes were tears. "I love Conrad, you have to know that. Do you know how long I've waited for a man to love me? I work here day after day and struggle to make my life happy and finally when I find someone to live in happiness with me, you tell me to leave him!"

"I just have a funny feeling about this," Susan said.

"But you don't know Conrad. You don't," she sniffed.

"I know and don't you find that strange?"

Jane leaned in again. Susan did the same.

"You've known this man since your vacation and so far, I've never met him."

"But he's a traveling man, Susan. He doesn't stay here often and when he does he just wants to be with me."

Susan breathed in deeply. The last thing she wanted was for her friend to bolt before she'd said everything she had come here to say.

"Please, Jane," she whispered, watching the children who were with her husband from the corner of her eye. She thought she saw him wink at her. "I love you, too and I want you to be happy. Perhaps if I met Conrad, sometime before the wedding, we could work through this."

"Oh, I don't know. He'll be coming in late the night before. I won't see him until then."

"Well, your love has to mean something. Ask him if you'd like to have dinner with your friend and her husband, get to know them a little. He couldn't object to that. Tell him you have the rest of your lives to be together."

"Maybe," Jane offered, taking Susan's hand. "Maybe I can do that. But, Susan, I'm not going to change my mind about marrying him. I can't."

***

Chris Clariton had been murdered with the same poison given to Bob, Kate and Chris' husband, David. It had happened two hours after she'd left Susan, at her old place. When the police found her, the house was bare of anything but the woman's body and a used paper cup.

"So, what happens next?" asked Susan, who was tired, following another tirade with her mother.

"I have no idea. All the clues are there, all the suspects in line, but the police still can't find Frank or Lane.

"None of the suspects have returned to the Kennedy house?"

"Not that they can determine and, as far as I know, they have undercover cops watching that place almost 24/7 now."

With four days before the wedding, Susan was chilled to the bone in more ways than one. Her mother was angry at her once again and William wasn't sharing anything new. Jane was excited. Susan had seen many of the decorations, centerpieces and other wedding hoopla. She'd smiled and given her best smile, though for whatever reason, Susan's heart was not in it—would probably never be in it.

Could a woman need a man so much to find happiness, that she was blind to the truth? What kind of man was Conrad Jackson, really and what, if anything did he have to do with the previous murders?

She and Henry wouldn't know until the eve before the wedding and that just had to be soon enough.

Frank

Hope was furious. No surprise there. As Susan sat on the sofa that Bob had been murdered on, she couldn't help but stare over at William. A small smile was hidden, she could see it, underneath his pressed and polished exterior.

"You saw that Chris Clariton woman just moments before her death?"

"I told you, Mother, two hours before she died."

"So, how did you do it?"

"Kill her?"

Hope pointed a finger at her daughter and all Susan could do was pretend that her mother's words weren't affecting her. But they were. And William was enjoying the exchange. If Susan lived to be a million years old, she'd never forget this day—the day her mother had blamed her for more than just Chris' murder.

"Why would I kill Chris?" Susan raved, intent on keeping glued to the couch, even though her mother walked the room like a raving lunatic, waving her arms.

"I don't know! How should I know that?"

"You're blaming me, isn't that fair enough?"

"Fair? I wouldn't call any of this—fair! You have ruined my happy marriage, brought the police into our happy lives—killed your sister—maybe not literally, but you must have said something. Bob told me all about your distance...when you were married and after. He told me about your secret meetings with Frank Olmstead, your friend Ms. Martha Boaz who practically lived on drugs. He told me everything you did. When he came here, unbelievably, he wanted to get back with you and sought my advice. I gave him what I could, but you've always been a hard-headed woman and I told him you'd probably be a hard egg to crack."

Susan felt the heat rise in her cheeks. "Do you remember that moment a couple of Christmases ago when you compared me to a hard-boiled egg?"

Hope stared over at her. "No."

"I do. You said something about me never being able to connect with a man. You placed an egg in my hand. When I asked if it was hard-boiled, I believe you said, 'It's as fresh as the moment the doctor placed you in my arms.' You proceeded to tell me that the egg you were holding was raw and that I could make my egg anyway I wanted it."

"Why would I say that?"

"You thought I could make my marriage work, even if love was no longer in the picture. But how is love best served? Scrambled? Sunny Side-Up? Over easy? Now, there's the answer."

"What's the answer?" Her mother's lips trembled.

"I didn't love Bob. And yes, I'd tried over and over again to make the marriage work. But he was too busy to return the favor, wasn't he, Mother? He was busy doing his swindling work and his spying work and his loafing around work—to really care about me. But you didn't care about that. You didn't care about my happiness, just that on the surface, everything looked *right*. Like the outside of a hard-boiled egg that was really raw inside, you wanted me to pretend that everything was alright!"

"Christian women should never divorce!"

The words rang in Susan's ears and made her wince. "And Christian mothers should never marry atheist men."

The words were cruel, Susan knew it. She regretted them the moment they'd been spoken. No matter that her mother had yelled at her and had always yelled at her. No matter that she didn't accept Henry and all he was for her. Now, suddenly, it all made sense. She'd divorced.

"So that's it. I divorced Bob and because of his sadness, his irreplaceable sadness, you blame me for his death, too."

"I do." The sob was quick. "You weren't here, but you did it just as if you were."

Susan's eyes were dripping with tears, but she barely noticed. She looked over at William and wished in that moment Henry was at her side. She didn't tell her mother that she'd considered William as the murderer of them all. She didn't tell her mother that William had her wrapped around his little finger and that she was less coherent than she'd ever seen her. She didn't say a word as she grabbed her coat and took a walk out the front door.

***

"I'm sorry," said Henry.

"What happened, Mom? Your eyes are all wet." Brianne reached for her.

"I'm fine."

"But you look sick. What's wrong with her, Dad?"

"She had a little argument with her mother today."

Oscar chewed his burrito and swallowed. "Figures," he said. "She's as crazy as a bat!

"Oscar!"

"Well, she is, Dad. As loony as a loon."

"What's a loon?" Brianne asked. "Is it a bird?"

Susan smiled. Leave it to her daughter to ease the tension. "As a matter of fact, yes. But your grandmother is not a bird, she is just having a hard time, that's all."

"What did she do?" Oscar asked.

Susan took a bite, swallowed, then reached for her glass. It would be sometime before she'd be able to speak to her mother again—if ever.

"She wasn't very nice to your mother."

"It's because of her husband," said Brianne, watching Susan's eyes. "He's a bad man."

Susan stared at her daughter. She'd probably heard some talk at some point, talk Susan now regretted. Brianne should have a good relationship with her grandmother, despite their lack of connection.

"Why do you say that?" asked Henry, wiping his mouth on the paper napkin.

"I think he's mean. He isn't nice to grandma."

"How do you know that?"

"She told me."

Susan blinked and tried to swallow, but the piece stuck firmly in her throat. She grabbed her glass, hoping to down it, but suddenly she couldn't breathe, she couldn't...

"Mom!" The sound of Brianne's voice floated above her head like an imagined specter. She felt Henry's hands and arms and the *pop!* that finally gave way.

Henry looked into her eyes. "Are you alright?" he asked.

"I was choking," she said.

"I know. You should never take a bite that big." He pointed to the piece of burrito. It sat innocently on her plate covered with saliva.

"Gross," Brianne said, pushing at the piece with her little finger. "Were you really choking, Mom?"

Susan gathered up her 10-year-old and held her close. "I was, but I'm fine now," she said.

***

"The police have located Frank," Henry said. They were sitting in front of the television and Brianne and her brother were munching their shared bag of popcorn on the floor.

"So, what is he saying?"

"They're not telling me. They just wanted to let me know he was in custody to relieve some stress."

"That's nice of them."

It was two days before the wedding and Susan still hadn't discussed with Henry how he really felt about taking *Honesty House* on full time. She just wasn't up to it.

Jane was beyond excited, she even had some good news for her. Yes, Conrad wanted to meet them. A thought had struck her then that Jane might have had a picture to show her—she hadn't even seen a wedding announcement come by—something she'd asked Jane about weeks ago only to get a sullen reply back.

"We're inviting everyone word of mouth. Conrad doesn't like his photo being taken, though he did say he would make an exception at the wedding."

Susan had thought it more than a little strange but had kept her mouth shut. She would just have to wait.

But as the hours passed before Jane's big day, all Susan could think about was how little she really knew her friend, especially now.

Everything was ready and as the day approached she grew even more worried. Should she tell the police what she knew? Or would the police wonder if, yet again, she was making a mountain out of a mole hill? Chris had been off center the last time they'd spoken before her death; had been off center every time they'd spoken before that. How could Susan be sure that the woman's ranting was not merely – delusional?

Red Lace

"What?"

"I told you, he's sick."

Sick in the head is more like it, Susan thought but didn't say.

"What about tomorrow? The wedding?"

"He says it's just nerves. He's excited for tomorrow." Jane grinned. "Oh, don't look so disappointed. You'll meet him tomorrow. What can one day matter?"

A lot, Susan thought again but didn't say.

"This is a nice place," Jane said, looking over at Henry. "Thanks."

"No problem." He looked over at Susan, winked once, then looked down at the menu. "I hear the pasta is marvelous here," he said.

***

Susan placed the white cloths on the tables and the white covers over the metal chairs. She hadn't seen Conrad yet, at least she didn't think so, but Jane was everywhere, seemingly—at once.

She'd chosen red roses for the occasion and napkins that looked like lace and plenty of greenery, "I want it to be like a garden," she said. The white taper candles filled each table and the place, once finished, looked strikingly like Cinderella's castle, at least the way Susan imagined it.

Still, no Conrad.

Henry wasn't there either and wouldn't be until right before the ceremony. Brianne and Oscar had been asked to be the flower girl and ring bearer, respectively, and they were both excited. But there was something in the air, something unmistakably—evil—that couldn't be removed from Susan's thoughts.

"So, he's feeling better today," she said, as her friend passed by, walk-running to the next project. The food needed to be set up and the punch bowl filled just before everyone arrived. The ceremony would be simple and sweet, according to Jane, and all Susan could think about was how funny she felt inside.

"Yes, much better!" Jane remarked as she raced by. "You won't have to wait much longer."

Suddenly, a funny thought, but not so funny really, came to her. What if there wasn't really a groom? What if all this time her friend had been in some sort of fantasy land, sort of like Chris had been when she'd told her that the marriage shouldn't take place.

But that was silly, wasn't it?

The chairs were ready and the podium where the preacher would stand, was set. Susan searched the room. There must be something she'd forgotten. She looked at the candles, the blessed table filled with the most scrumptious delicacies she'd ever seen—her friend, or maybe Conrad—had wanted escargot.

A half an hour to take off, so to speak, friends began to arrive. Jane's parents had excused themselves from attending at the last minute, but there seemed plenty of friends, some she knew, some she didn't, to fill in the chairs she'd swathed with the white fabric, a large bow at the back.

Everything looked beautiful—really—the sights, the smells, the music—Jane had vied for a small band and they had arrived just moments earlier and just in time, too, before her loved ones had begun to arrive.

And then she saw him.

At first, she was unsure that it was him, she'd had to look twice. He appeared to be evading her, standing behind drapery and white linen backdrops, but then, there he was again, taking her friend by the hands and gazing into her eyes.

Lane Kennedy.

The shock of seeing him stunned her. Lane Kennedy? Why was he here? Why was he holding her friend's hands?

She had little time to process the shock. Her mother was suddenly beside her. "So, is there any special place we should sit?"

"No... wherever you want."

William smiled. The smile was vacant and shallow. He turned to his wife and led her to a chair.

Susan turned back in the direction of the white curtains where she'd first seen them, but emptiness grabbed at her heart instead. What was Lane Kennedy doing here? Again, the thought plagued her mind and her heart pounded and wouldn't stop pounding, even as everyone arrived and the chairs filled.

Moments later, when she heard her husband and children's voices, she forced a smile to her lips. They couldn't know she was afraid. Turning, she saw no one but her husband. "Where are the children?" she asked.

"Back there..."

"What?" Her heart stopped cold. She thought of Kennedy in the same instant. No, they couldn't be...

Henry looked at her quizzically.

"Lane Kennedy is here," she whispered. "He is—here."

"Lane Kennedy?"

"I think he's pretending to be Conrad Jackson. And I think..." Susan paused. "I think something else is going to happen today *besides* a wedding."

Henry's face grew pale. His eyes searched in the direction the children had gone.

"Are you alright?" she asked.

"I don't know. I sent the children to get ready..."

Susan tried to breath evenly. "Where?"

"There, right behind the white curtain. I think that's Brianne's feet."

Susan looked in the direction of her husband's pointing finger. "I'm going," she said.

"The children need to stand at the front of the line," Jane was saying when she approached. "Right there." She was aglow. The dress, a perfect Cinderella rendition, flowed at her feet.

Susan looked down the line. Everyone appeared ready to begin—even her children. They smiled up at her.

"Where is...Conrad?" Susan asked. Good, Henry was here, standing right where he needed to be standing, beside her.

"That man is so funny. He just ran to the restroom. We'll get started as soon as he gets back." She looked down at Brianne and over at Oscar. "Your children look fine," she said, taking Susan's hand. "I can hardly believe my day has finally arrived!"

Tears glinted in Susan's eyes. What could she possibly—say?

"You can't marry Conrad. You can't!" Her voice was too loud, she knew it, but the words had to be said.

"What are you talking about?" Jane answered, searching her friend's eyes. "I'm getting married!"

Henry touched Jane's arm. "Listen to Susan," he said.

"Listen? You two are crazy! Conrad is in love with me and I, him."

Susan blinked as Lane Kennedy entered the room. He walked to his soon-to-be bride. "So sorry," he began, taking a brief look at Henry and herself. "Why, these must be your friends, the ones you've been telling me about."

A creepy feeling, unlike the sheer dark of winter, entered Susan's soul. She could barely look at him.

"This is Susan and her husband, Henry."

"Susan. Henry." He reached out his hand. "Pleased to meet you both. Jane has told me so much about you." The man was pleasant, even too pleasant if that was possible. He looked into Susan's eyes and she saw something there, something she couldn't explain.

"Now that you've met Conrad, can you please take a seat. I want to get married."

Susan's fingers tingled. "No! You can't have my children!" she screamed.

Henry touched her arm. "You go. I'll stand back here and watch them until everyone is out."

"A worried mother?" Lane Kennedy asked, a smile creasing his face.

"She always gets a little tense when she has to leave the children for more than a few short minutes." Henry pushed her slightly to the main room. "Don't worry," he said, "I have everything under control."

Susan couldn't believe it. What was her Henry doing? As she shakily walked back out she saw that her mother and William were staring at her. In fact, many at the wedding were staring at her. The only seat left was near the back.

But she didn't sit there. She couldn't—sit. Grabbing her phone from her purse she walked to a nearby door and made a phone call, perhaps the most important phone call she'd ever made.

The wedding procession started. Her children were beautiful—even Oscar, who remembered to offer the bride's ring at just the right time.

Lane Kennedy stared lovingly at his bride and as he finished his vow and she hers, there was a loud crash from the kitchen. Or was it a crash? It was loud whatever it was.

She blinked over at her children. They stood off to one side as the couple kissed. Maybe she'd been wrong. Maybe everything was going to be okay.

But something was terribly wrong. She'd noticed it on the dress first, a large red spot and then it was on her friend's hand...

Someone screamed—it sounded just like Brianne. Other screams followed and before she knew it, Susan was racing to the front of the room.

A police officer was suddenly in their midst, brushing past the preacher and grabbing hold of Lane Kennedy.

"Go, to the back of the room!" Susan shouted. "Now!" Oscar grabbed his sister's hand and together they ran in the general direction of the punch bowl.

Susan knelt by the side of her dear friend.

"Jane! Jane!" She tried to stop the gush that was quickly changing the color of her friend's white dress—to red.

"Shut the doors! No one is to leave this room!" someone shouted.

Susan shuddered. Her friend was as pale and still—as death.

***

Brianne was crying. Susan tried to sooth her but her words had little effect. Where was Henry? She hadn't seen him since before the gun shot and now, all of them were huddled with loved ones. .

Where was Henry?

Oscar stared blankly in front of him. "I'm worried about grandma," he said. "Where is she?"

Susan looked to the beginning row of chairs. Her mother was huddled in William's arms."There," she pointed.

Oscar nodded. "Where's Dad?" he asked.

"I'm not sure," she said, the only answer she could give at such a moment.

"Want some punch?" Oscar nodded. He poured some of the liquid into a glass cup and handed it to her. "I was going to pour some earlier for Brianne but I wasn't sure if it had alcohol in it or not."

Susan reached for the cup and smelled it. Well, it definitely wasn't laced with alcohol. The consistency was thicker than she remembered someone pouring into the bowl just minutes before the wedding had begun, however. It didn't smell funny, but the hairs on her arms stood up.

There he was, sitting on the sofa, about to take a similar sip from someone who had kindly offered him a drink. She sat the cup on the table. "Go and get a police officer," she said to Oscar.

Oscar looked over at her. "Aren't you going to drink the punch?"

"No." She pour the liquid back into the bowl. "Go and get a police officer like I asked."

He nodded and Susan looked down at Brianne who was still whimpering. "Look," she said at last, "we're going to get through this. Don't worry."

"What about your friend? Is she dead?"

"I don't know."

"Why wouldn't you drink the punch?"

"I'm not sure, but we're going to sit here until we know what's going on."

***

"Henry!" Susan collapsed in her husband's arms.

"Are you alright?"

She nodded. "You?"

"Fine."

Oscar stood near him.

"Where's the police officer?" she asked.

"I found Dad instead," he said, smiling. "That's okay, isn't it?"

Susan smiled. "Sit down next to your sister for a minute—don't let her drink any punch—I've got to talk to Dad."

She stood. "I can't be sure but I think there might be something wrong with the punch."

"Really, what?" He leaned in.

"Don't even touch it."

He blinked at her. "Lane Kennedy has been taken away and I thought you'd want to know the condition of Jane," he said.

"How is..."

"She's been taken to the hospital—she's still breathing—at last check-in. Your mom seems fine, too, though William is in sore shape. They found a gun on him."

Susan held Henry close. "I knew it," she said.

"Your mother is going to need someone," Henry said.

"I know that, too," Susan answered, looking in the direction of her mother. She was sitting alone now, balled up like a tiny baby.

"I think someone may have laced the punch with antifreeze. It's just a feeling."

Henry was momentarily taken aback. "Wouldn't surprise me," he said, looking down into the punch bowl. "I hope no one has had any yet."

"Well, I someone poured the punch out just before the ceremony began. Everyone was sitting in anticipation then, but I wasn't watching the punch bowl the entire time so..."

"I need to let the police know. Keep guard until I get back."

***

Her mother wouldn't be consoled and five hours later, after the room had been checked over by police and everyone had been questioned, including monitoring their current health for poisoning, the wedding guests—anyone who'd had punch before the ceremony— were sent on to the hospital for further observation.

Susan, Henry and the children arrived home near 1 a.m. She called the hospital but Jane was still in the emergency room. No one would tell her a thing except that the two wedding participants who'd had a bit of the punch were going to be fine.

"Do you think you can watch the children? I need to see Jane," she said, taking off her fancy dress and sliding on a pair of jeans and a T-shirt.

"Oh, no you don't. I don't need you getting stressed over there."

"But I have to."

Henry patted the bed. She sat next to him. He was already in his pajamas. "I know you love her but there's nothing you can do. They won't let you in there, you're just going to have to wait it out. Gunshot wounds are nothing to write home about."

"Then when?" She hadn't meant to whine, but there it was.

"Tomorrow. Oscar can stay home with Brianne and we can make a visit."

"I won't be able to sleep."

"I know. At least change your clothes and get into bed. I can help you with the rest."

"What's that supposed to mean?"

"Not what you're thinking. Now get your pajamas on. I'll give you a nice back rub. Oh, and before I forget. I knew something was up with this Conrad, so, before the wedding, I went into the police station and told them what we'd heard from Chris Clariton. They actually believed me, but I think this was only because they'd been receiving some new information that matched hers from the one and only Frank Olmstead."

Susan smiled slightly, snuggling under the covers glad for some warmth, worried about her children so far away in their own rooms. But the windows were locked and the doors bolted. And Jane? She wasn't sure, but Susan prayed silently that she would be okay.

***

Jane was pale but alive. The five-minute drive by ambulance to a trauma center—had saved her life. As she reached out her hand to Susan, Susan took it and squeezed it gently. A wound to the abdomen was a horrible thing, but she'd reached the hospital just in time and for this, Susan was grateful.

"I should have listened to you," Jane said.

"That doesn't matter now. Just get well."

"Conrad...I thought..."

"I know. You deserve to be loved."

"I thought I was going to die."

Susan smiled down at her friend. They'd been through a lot and not all of it had been easy. But it wasn't the end for either one of them.

"I guess I won't be leaving *Honesty House* after all," her friend said.

Susan smiled. "I don't know what we'd do without you," she answered.

***

A handful of things were sure. The punch bowl had indeed been laced with antifreeze.

William had shot the gun that had wounded and almost killed, Jane.

And Frank was careful to make sure that if it *wasn't for him*, no one would have ever known anything. Susan could just imagine his buggy eyes flapping as he finally revealed all to the police.

Still, questions remained unanswered. Why had Lane Kennedy married Jane? Who had killed Bob and her sister, as well as David and his wife, Chris? And why?

Months later, the pieces were beginning to sort themselves. Her mother had begun to heal, though she was tight lipped and not very forthcoming to any questions or concerns about her health. Perhaps she needed time.

Before long, it was summer and the cold wind had changed to a pleasantly warm breeze. It was spring before everything came to the surface—spring before her husband began his new detective agency and Brianne sat at his feet listening to 'mystery' stories. She was eleven by then and as pretty as the days were long.

Oscar was fourteen by the time they found out he was secretly dating a girl. Oh, they would meet her, that was for sure, but right now just wasn't the right time.

Jane was getting on famously at *Honesty House*, almost back to her old self the day Susan arrived for lunch. They spoke of old times and the days when innocence was the rule rather than the exception.

And Susan spoke about Ephraim Humphrey. "That man was taking his revenge out on me, did you know that?"

When Jane nodded her head, Susan continued: "I can hardly believe it myself. Even locked away he was still masterminding his revenge, trying to get back at me for putting him in prison. Killing four people, almost five, is a lot to take revenge on—even for him."

"So, who did he get to do his dirty work?"

"You saw the news."

Jane frowned. "I didn't, at least not all of it. I know it's got something to do with William, your mom's ex, but I don't know the details. I heard some talk but I could never bring myself to watch the news."

Susan understood, though she hoped her friend would one day free herself completely of the shooting and the man she had loved.

"William married my mother to get to me. He wanted to kill Bob—he'd been my husband after all and he'd swindled him out of all that money—but Kate had actually beaten him to it. Evidently, Bob had tired of loneliness and had decided to spend some time with his college friends—just this once—and that was where the laced drink was first poured. Only Kate had placed the cup—a cup that had been meant for her—in front of Bob not knowing it had been meant for her. William must have about died himself seeing that.

"So that's why he was found dead on the couch? But there was a cup there, too."

Susan nodded. "William confessed to bringing it along and planting it just where it needed to be planted to create the whole suicide thing. The note that he'd convinced Bob to write that very night, had only cinched the deal. The truth is, Bob had actually decided he wanted to start over."

She looked over at her friend and seeing that she was taking the news in stride continued:

"Because William's first try to kill Kate had bungled, William knew he needed to try again. But when and where? And then it came to him. Because Kate was convinced he was finally going to marry her—they could toast to the occasion, laced wine and all."

"What about your mother?"

"Divorce, I guess. Then he'd be free to marry Kate—or so she thought."

"That's terrible. I'm so sorry, Susan."

Susan touched her friend's hand.

Henry had been physically shaken when he'd told Susan the details, but in the end, she'd thanked him. It was better to know.

Kate had been an easy mark for William, she loved him, but the last two killings had been a bit harder to orchestrate, though William had done what was necessary to protect his own hide. The

group—such as it was—was breaking up and he would be blamed for everything.

"But what about me? Why would he want to kill—me?" Jane asked.

"Lane Kennedy's doing, of course. He wanted total revenge and that total revenge included taking my best friend's life, as well as everyone else in that room, including me."

"Oh, gosh," Jane said. "Can you ever forgive me for not believing you?"

"Sure."

She clasped Susan's hand.

"So, William was the father of Kate's child, then?"

"No. Evidently Kate had a boyfriend—not a very worthy one I'm afraid—who knew nothing about what was really going on with Kate."

"How could a man like Ephraim Humphrey wield such power? I mean, he's in prison, after all, why would William be willing to do any of his bidding?"

"Lots of money. Millions in fact, promised to those who did as he demanded. That man has more pot holes with hidden money in them than rats with secret hiding places."

Jane laughed and then her countenance grew sad. "I only wish Conrad had been the man he put himself out to be. I really loved him." The tenderness in Jane's eyes was unmistakable. She wiped them quickly, squeezing Susan's hand. "You know what? I'm up for a grand adventure, aren't you? How about a leisurely visit to the local craft fair? I've just been dying to decorate my place for Saint Patrick's Day."

"No kidding."

Jane stood, pressing Susan into a tight hug. "You know you mean everything to me," she said, wrapping her arm around Susan's shoulders and walking her out. "And I'm bound and determined to prove it."

Delicious Deviled Eggs

Makes 12 halves

Place 6 eggs in pot big enough that they line the bottom.
Fill pot with cold water at least two inches above eggs.
Bring to a full rolling boil.
Turn off heat and cover.
Let set for 20 minutes, pour off hot water.
Cover with cold water and ice and let set for 20 minutes in cold water.
Egg yolks turn greenish if not cooled quickly enough.
Peel eggs.
Cut lengthwise, putting yolks in small mixing bowl and whites on a tray.
Mash yolks up with a fork and add
> A dab of mustard (just less than a tablespoon)
> 3-4 drops of Tabasco sauce
> 1 teaspoon of Worcestershire sauce
> Two tablespoons of mayonnaise
> Salt and pepper to taste

Either use a teaspoon or decorating set to place the yolk mixture into the whites. I like to use the large star pattern with my cake decorating bag; it makes them look extra pretty.
Sprinkle with paprika.
Cover lightly and refrigerate.